# The Museum Mysteries
## & other short stories
*by*
# Glyn Idris Jones

First Published in Greece 2012
© Glyn Jones 2010
The author's moral rights have been asserted.

Douglas Foote

ISBN 978-960-9610-00-1

www.dcgmediagroup.com

# Contents

Publishers note                                     iv
Mr Nicholson's Justice                               1
Inyoni                                               9
The Dream                                           21
Antjie Somers                                       31
Pioneer                                             37
Another Christmas Carol                             43
The Museum Mysteries                                59

# Publishers note

*S*hort stories are an often neglected part of a writer's repertoire, but as with much of the larger works available, they can be just as witty, inventive and entertaining.

This collection spans the writing career of Glyn Jones from his early works in the late 1950's of *Antjie Somers* and *Inyoni*, stories which draw on traditional myths of his upbringing in South Africa, to the most recent: *Museum Mysteries* a full Gothic horror novella.

These stories, spanning over sixty years, show the development of Glyn Jones' writing style when seen as a collective whole.

We hope you enjoy them.

Douglas Foote.

# Mr Nicholson's Justice

*M*y uncle said that Mister Nicholson was the reincarnation of an Egyptian High Priest or Cesare Borgia, or some other recognised historical master of cunning and cruelty, for he has the craftiest face imaginable and his long spindly legs seemed to impress upon one the full implications of Caesar's phrase, 'Yon Cassius has a lean and hungry look!'

He was most certainly lean, though if ever he looked hungry, we were hardly to blame, for he was extremely well fed and contented. So much so in fact, that he seldom took much interest in birds and small furry creatures, except to follow their every movement with his wicked green eyes. We never knew him to be cruel after the manner of his species and, until the incident I am about to relate (except for his Machiavellian countenance), we had not the slightest reason for supposing him cunning.

We did not doubt he was a highly intelligent animal for he had proved that to us in numerous ways. For instance, if he was inside the house and wished to go out, or outside and wanted to come in; a state of affairs perpetually requested from a soft plaintive wail to louder tones demanding immediate attention, regaining admittance sometimes required the intelligence of which I was speaking.

It so happened that the knocker on our door was placed low

and to one side. Why anyone should have wanted it there in the first place I cannot imagine but Mister Nicholson found the position most convenient and had learnt to use it with telling effect, for by standing on a ledge beside the door and leaning against the wall, he was able to stretch up and lift the knocker, allowing it to drop with a sharp rap. This operation continued at frequent and regular intervals until in exasperation someone let him in. According to a neighbour he once spent a whole afternoon at this little game not realising the family were away and, when we eventually returned, he resembled an athlete at the end of a gruelling marathon. I do not think he ever forgave us.

Apart from food, sleep, and door rapping, Mister Nicholson had one passion in life and that was for his friend Lollop, a large and sprightly Belgian hare who lived in a hutch at the bottom of the garden.

What caused the bond of affection between these two we never understood, but maybe it is not meant for human beings to understand the sometimes peculiar friendships that spring up in the animal kingdom. We concluded that, being members of the same household, they had decided to live in amity together, or had united in a common front against their next door neighbour, a rather savage and muscular bull terrier named Pickles who spent most of his time staring at them from between the slats in the fence, rather like a young spiv at any street corner admiring the passing of a shapely ankle.

Pickles was a pedigree animal whose family had acquired over a number of years a small fortune in silver and bronze and, like most pedigreed beasts he was temperamental, excitable, and quickly responsive to external stimuli. We thought rather highly of him, being authorities on these matters, although we were extremely careful never to approach too close, bull terriers being above all things strictly one man dogs and feeling we provided enough stimulus to rouse his worst nature. I hardly think it reasonable that we could impress upon a cat and a rabbit that dogs will be dogs. To them, no dog is a good dog, and Lollop for one was terrified of the creature. It was probably just as well that during the day Pickles was chained to his kennel, and at night when allowed to roam at will, Lollop was safe in his hutch, and Mister Nicholson beneath the kitchen stove. The interest the dog showed in the animals was a little disconcerting at first, especially when he whined eagerly and scratched at the fence but after a while they became accustomed to his presence and, although it seemed he would have been pleased to join their fun, he never received an invitation and we could not help feeling his nose was badly put out of joint. Sooner or later he was bound to try and gate crash the party and we did not like to dwell on the possible consequences.

It was a source of endless delight to both family and their guests to sit at the study window and watch the pets as they played, and numerous were the games invented. The one achieving greatest popularity with both spectators and participants alike was a type of animal free for all which provided hours of good clean fun. The pair would chase each other about the lawn, twisting and turning, leaping, rolling, sidestepping, trying desperately to shake off a determined pursuer. If Lollop being the quarry, found it impossible to escape the unwelcome attentions of Mister Nicholson's teeth about his ankles, he would apply the brakes suddenly, lift his hind legs, and deal the cat such a mighty blow in the face that he would career about the lawn in anguish, the triumphant Lollop hard on his heels. Mister Nicholson, now finding the position reversed, and not being the possessor of a strong pair of hind legs, would make a bee line for the old pear tree and shin up it for all he was worth. Lollop, seeing only the fleeing cat before him, and incensed by the chase, little realised his danger until too late and was brought to an abrupt halt by barking his pink nose painfully on the trunk of the tree. This made them quits and the whole object of the game was to see who could bump whose nose the hardest and most often until, exhausted, they would lie down together and go to sleep.

Then, one night came tragedy, and at first it seemed hardly creditable that the fun and games were over.

On a beautiful sunny morning I entered the garden as usual to let Lollop out of his cage when to my consternation I found the hutch door wide open and no sign of the hare. The party had been gate crashed, and my worst fears were justified when I found him behind the tool shed, sprawled on top of the compost heap: he had been torn to pieces!

Mister Nicholson, who had accompanied me in high spirits, approached the carcase warily, sniffed it, and touched it gingerly with his paw. Then ,without a sound, he returned to the house, the tip of his black tail flicking swiftly; ominously.

I realise the bull terrier must have scrambled over the fence during the night and somehow managed to open the hutch, and I buried Lollop in the compost heap where he and Mister Nicholson had taken the sun so often.

It was a sad blow to the household, and although we keenly felt the death of Lollop, Mister Nicholson refused to be consoled over the loss of a friend and went completely of his food. The choicest and daintiest morsels were placed to no avail. He spent his day crouched on the fence above Pickle's kennel and never took his gaze from the dog's face. At first the terrier barked excitedly and strained towards the cat but after a while his barking subsided to a menacing growl which in turn disappeared as he settled down under the baleful scrutiny and obviously decided to ignore it. But as the days passed it proved too much and he became increasingly restless and uneasy. We tried unsuccessfully to catch Mister Nicholson, but he made off hastily whenever we approached only to return as soon as we left. We tried to entice him with food and terms of endearment but he was not interested. He grew ragged and scrawny but he maintained his lonely vigil, and although the neighbours complained whenever they saw him, there was nothing we could do except wait for hunger to drive him in.

The dog's kennel was moved and Mister Nicholson moved with it, always sitting just out of reach. Finally we gave up the struggle. Apart from shooting there seemed no way out except to let events take their course. The kennel was moved back to it's original position, Mister Nicholson returned to the fence, and we settled down to await the climax to this game of patience.

On the sixth day it came. The terrier, no longer able to stand the silent third degree, turned suddenly ferocious and with the strength that mad things seem to have he made a desperate lunge toward his tormentor. It was all Mister Nicholson had been waiting for. The length of chain preventing the dog from attaining his full leap and his snapping jaws were stopped short, a good eight inches below the top of the fence. The cat responded swiftly. One long paw flashed out. The soft pads unsheathed their lethal, razor sharp hooks to slash viciously across the dogs face, and he fell to the ground a yelping, howling heap of agony. Mister Nicholson jumped down into his own territory, stretched lazily in the sun, washed his paws, and strolled sedately into the kitchen where he promptly lapped up a plate of milk and mewed politely for more.

Pickles was destroyed. A blind dog is a liability to anyone, and although it created a lot of bad feeling and in the end cost us a pretty penny, Mister Nicholson remained singularly unperturbed. Revenge must have been sweet and I suppose he considered it to be no more than his justice!

# Inyoni

*F*never learned his real name, where he came from, or how he arrived on my farm, but there he was early one morning as I set out from the house to begin the day's work, squatting on his haunches in front of the stoep with his arms folded over his knees and looking for all the world like an old black crow! He was dressed in an amazing assortment of feathers and strips of thong, and about his neck hung a medicine horn, a bottle on a length of string and an old bead message, probably given to him many years before by a lover or a wife. His shiny bald pate was crowned by an old man's clay ring from the back of which dangled a small goat's bladder, and the skin on his ancient legs, grey with dirt, looked cracked and parchment-like as he sat scrabbling his toes in the dust.

On my appearance he lifted a wizened arm to touch his forehead in solemn greeting and rather taken aback by the sight of him, I returned his salutation with a curt nod. I asked him what he wanted but his only response was to show his gums in a toothless smile, his sharp little eyes disappearing behind the thousand wrinkles that creased his face.

A group of boys stood close by, gazing at him curiously and whispering to themselves.

'What does this old man want?' I asked them.

'He says he wants work, Baas.'

'An old man like this?' I laughed. 'What work can he do? He should be sitting in the sun outside his kraal drinking beer!'

'He says he is a milk boy, Baas.'

The old man followed our conversation with interest but he volunteered no further information. His black eyes darted towards the boys and back again as he waited for an answer. I must have been born with a tender heart, for although I had no need for a milk boy at that time, the little creature seemed so pathetic that, against my better judgement, I decided to give him a trial. I told my head boy to take care of him and see him started that evening.

We named him "Inyoni," which means, "bird."

Whether it was one of the boys or myself who first called him that I can't remember but he looked so much like a bird it seemed the most natural name for him. It was afterwards pointed out to me that there is sometimes very little difference between the eyes of a bird and those of a snake.

From the first his work was satisfactory and as time passed I noticed that the cows he handled were giving more milk than ever before. I attributed this to the gentleness and I think one of the reasons why I grew to like the old boy was his sympathetic and easy manner with cattle. I would often hear him crooning over them as he milked, or sucking the air in between his gums in a soothing hiss. He never spoke to me and I do not recall ever having heard him utter a single word more to any of the boys.

I kept only a few head of cattle, grade cows for the most, and it was my custom to personally supervise the milking each day. I knew every cow by name and grew quite fond of them, spoke to them and made little shows of affection, and I felt that they in turn knew and were fond of me. One in particular was a great favourite of mine, and usually came in for a little more attention than the others. Her name was Jezebel: a docile beast and a good milker; besides which she had calved four beautiful heifers which raised her considerably in my estimation.

One evening while doing my rounds I strolled as usual into her stall, patting her rump as was my habit, when suddenly she turned her head at my touch and without warning kicked out viciously, catching me a glancing blow on the shin that sent me reeling against the side of the stall, where she pressed me with her body as she backed out, trying to get me with her horns. I yelled frantically for the boys who came running at my cry and beat the animal off, as I staggered out trembling with shock. The incident struck me as most peculiar, but as Jezebel was in calf at the time I though no more of it and attributed her lack of manners to expectant motherhood. It was only after a second animal tried the same trick that I had a sneaking suspicion all was not well, and my suspicions were confirmed one evening as I sat on the stoep having my usual after dinner pipe and coffee. My head boy came to the bottom of the steps and asked if could speak to me. I nodded, and after a moment's hesitation he began.

'Baas, it is Inyoni!'

'Yes Petrus, and what of Inyoni?'

'Baas, Inyoni is bad, Baas!'

I realised he needed a little coaxing and I nodded in encouragement but after a lengthy silence during which he never once looked at me but allowed his gaze to wander in every direction I grew a little impatient and prodded him.

'Bad?'

'Yes, Baas!'

For a moment I couldn't help smiling at his reticence but this was getting us nowhere. It is the local custom to arrive at the point of a discussion by the most devious route and if time and patience permit it is best to let them do so, but that evening I was in no mood for beating about the bush. I thumbed the tobacco in my pipe with a gesture of annoyance.

'And just what is bad about Inyoni?' I asked.

'Baas, that I do not know, but we do not like him; we would like to see him go.'

Now Petrus had been my head boy ever since I bought the farm a few years back and I knew I could rely on his integrity. I had never known him to be afraid before but, whatever it was about Inyoni that was upsetting him, I could see he was too scared to speak of it. Admittedly the old chap was a somewhat frightening character, probably even more so to superstitious boys, with his sharp little eyes and cunning leer and dressed up for all the world like a witch doctor but, after having experienced his work I would be sorry to lose him, he had such a way with the animals.

Witch doctor! A way with cows! I mused a while. The cows certainly seemed to be behaving in a most unusual fashion. I felt a little ashamed of the whole idea, it seemed so fantastic and I tried to laugh it off, but Petrus was in no mood for laughing and hung his head dolefully.

'Come now, Petrus, you don't think Inyoni is a witch doctor do you?' I asked him, half embarrassed and smiling a little at his mournful appearance.

'No, Baas, maybe not a witch doctor, but he must go or I go, and the rest of the boys; they go also.'

He was obviously deeply troubled and there was something quite ominous in his attitude.

I placed my coffee cup on the table and stood up hastily. This was nothing short of blackmail and I was angry. There was not a worker on my farm could tell me what and what not to do. On the other hand I had enough trouble procuring labour as it was and could not run the risk of losing a dependable bunch. I walked down the steps and stood facing him.

'If you would give me one good reason for getting rid of Inyoni, instead of coming to me with children's tales about being bad, and no proof of anything bad having happened, or likely to happen, I may consider it. You are a Christian aren't you?'

He looked at me rather startled and nodded.

'And hasn't the umfundees told you not to be afraid of witch doctors and witch doctors medicine?'

He nodded again, rather miserably, and rubbing the top of one bare foot against his shin, lowered his head.

'I am not afraid, Baas, but Inyoni must go.'

He was adamant, and there seemed nothing for it but to get rid of the bone of contention before I had a mutiny on my hands. I told Petrus to let Inyoni know he could collect his wages first thing in the morning and wished him a surly good night.

But in the morning Inyoni did not come and I found him in the cow shed milking Jezebel, as usual crooning all the while to her in his cracked piping voice. He took no notice of my presence or of what I said, and it became obvious that he considered the farm his home, and was not prepared to shift for anybody. I informed him rather curtly that as I had given him notice, if he was not off my property by sundown, I would have him arrested as a trespasser. Whether or not he heard this ultimatum I cannot tell, but that day seemed to drag interminably and I found myself continually thinking of him and wondering whether he had decided to move. When the cook called me in for morning coffee he was still there, and when I went up for lunch I saw him squatting in the sun outside the compound. In the evening he returned to his milking.

I was reluctant to be harsh with the old man but the others were becoming increasingly restless and I sensed there was trouble brewing. I telephoned Sergeant Nel in charge of the local police station to ask his advice.

'You leave it to me,' he said, after I had explained the situation. 'I know his type well enough. I'll come out right now.'

'Thanks,' I answered, 'but take it easy, hey?'

I had experienced police methods before and was not happy about this.

Nel arrived some time later, trotting down to the house on a beautiful chestnut gelding, a horse that was the envy of the neighbourhood, and which had earned him the highest reputation in gymkhana meets up and down the country. He was a brilliant rider, polo player and judge of horse flesh, and like many people who shine in some particular field, a vain and conceited man. I had very little time for him though. He was coarse, boastful, arrogant, and notorious for his cruelty to prisoners. Many farmers openly condoned this treatment believing that the only way to treat savages is with savagery, and those who objected to it thought it expedient to remain silent so he was well received in agricultural and sporting circles.

He was accompanied by a native constable who was sent off to make the arrest while I invited him in for a cup of coffee. We chatted about local affairs and the prospects of the hunting season and over our second cup I told him why I had dismissed the old boy.

'But I am sorry to see him go,' I added. 'He was a good worker and I cannot imagine what the other have against him. He seems quite harmless to me.'

He shrugged his shoulders and putting down his cup prepared to leave.

'What does it matter?' he said. 'If he is a nuisance we must get rid of him, whether you like it or not.'

I followed him outside to where Inyoni was sitting, guarded by the native constable. This time there was no arm raised in greeting for his wrists were cuffed; only his eyes flashed anger and hatred as he sat in the pool of yellow light cast by a paraffin lamp. Beyond the perimeter of light I could see shadows of my workers, flitting in the darkness, or standing motionless as they watched our every move.

Nel stood talking for a moment and then, mounting his horse, ordered the constable to follow with the prisoner, and the trio set off. I never saw Inyoni again. He died and was buried three days later, and the autopsy revealed the causes of death being natural!

After he had gone the boys returned to their work singing happily and life resumed its old course. I had a good year all told, the only tragedy being the loss of Jezebel who died giving birth to a bull calf. He was a fine little animal though and as I would soon have need of another bull I decided to keep him.

****

It was just a year later: one morning as I left the house I suddenly thought I saw Inyoni sitting by the stoep. The image was so vivid I was brought to an abrupt halt as my heart missed a beat. Good grief, it gave me a turn! I am not a very imaginative fellow and it is not like me to be seeing things!

I entered the cow shed half expecting to see him milking Jezebel and throughout the day I had the uncanny feeling that he was present. Once or twice I shuddered and looked around hastily, like a child in the dark, but of course there was nothing and as the boys seemed as gay and cheerful as ever, the feeling gradually wore off.

That night the trouble began. Jezebel's calf broke out of his camp and the following morning one of the boys found him drowned in the deep mud surrounding the dam. Only his tail and a patch of rump were showing and when we dragged him out we found the skin on his belly ripped to shreds from barbed wire. Within the next fortnight two more cows died in this same mysterious fashion and four boys quit. I was worried. There was no explanation for the animals' breakouts, but as some of the others bore lacerations from the wire where they had obviously been pressed against the fence before it snapped, I could only presume that something was frightening them, and frightening them pretty badly.

I erected a secondary fence around the dam and one night set Petrus on watch.

In the early hours of the morning I was awakened by a violent hammering on the door and cries of, 'Baas! Baas!'

It was Petrus, excited and trembling, and gabbling about some strange cow that had got into the camp and was chasing the others as though it were mad. I dressed hurriedly and grabbing my rifle we headed out toward the camp. The moon was high, flooding the world with silver, and it was easy to follow the path at a good steady trot. We hurried along, Petrus panting hard at my heels, and I must confess it was comforting to have another human being with me. All was quiet when we eventually reached the camp, the cattle either dozing or grazing peacefully. I cast a glance at Petrus, breathing hard and still trembling, his eyes rolling from side to side as he crouched beside me pointing to the far end of the field.

We hurried across, hardly pausing to inspect the broken fence, and ran down to the dam. The precautionary fence I had built was smashed as well, two poles having been torn from the ground, and above the mud we could see the hindquarters of a cow still kicking and twitching spasmodically. I sat down in the damp grass, gripping my rifle between my knees, and laid my forehead on it's cool barrel. At that moment I wanted to weep, not only because of the loss I could hardly sustain, but from the sheer agony of helplessness. Whatever was causing this havoc I was determined to find it out and the following night both Petrus and I kept watch with two more boys guarding the end of the field nearest the dam.

The night passed peacefully enough, but as the early hours of the morning approached a slight breeze rustled through the grass causing me to pull my collar higher and shake the chill from my shoulders. The moon rose over the far hills bathing the countryside in her soft light and at the same time Petrus tugged at my sleeve and whispered urgently, 'There she is Baas, look there!'

I followed the direction of his pointing finger and froze in horror for the cow that had suddenly appeared was no ordinary animal. I could never be more certain of any beast as I could of Jezebel – and this was Jezebel!

The cattle seemed to sense her at the same time and trotted about uneasily. Fascinated I watched her manoeuvre them skilfully into a bunch, then lowering her head she charged. The two boys fled for their lives before the panic stricken herd and with the instinct born of despair I lifted my rifle and fired – twice. The echoes died away into the night and of Jezebel there was no sign. The cattle were still milling about in panic but with nothing to drive them there was no break through and nothing further happened that night.

In the morning the remaining boys packed their bags and left; all except Petrus, he stayed on for a while. But the farm had earned its reputation and I could get no one to work so in the end I paid him off and pulled out. There was little else I could do. The storms I could fight; hail and frost, locust and drought. One season's failure meant another's hard work.

But who can fight the memory of a little black figure with flashing eyes and a cunning smile? A little figure called Inyoni!

# The Dream

"*H*e's got to change it," I said to myself. "It's imperative, he's just got to change it!"

I don't know how long I had been walking, an hour maybe? Two? Three? I couldn't remember. I couldn't even remember coming out of the house. But I did remember the dream. I wondered what the time was and looked at my wrist but it appeared I had even forgotten my watch. Now that was a stupid thing to do, to come out without my watch. Maybe I was late; in too much of a hurry, but late for what? Oh, yes! I remember. I had to see him and see him quickly. I had to persuade him about the dream. The dream! That was it… the dream! Now where could I have left my watch? How long had I been walking? I couldn't remember, couldn't think clearly anymore.

I looked around vaguely, trying to get my bearings. I was off Baker Street somewhere. A quick walk to Harley Street and then I could tell him. "Doctor," I'd say, "it's the dream!" No, no, I mustn't think about it now; wait till I see him I'll only get more confused. A short walk to Harley Street and by the time I get there he will have arrived; then I can tell him. It will be all right.

The heavy brass knocker; a lion's head with a ring in it's mouth was icy to the touch. The glossy black door reflected the movements of the passers by. She answered it as she always answered it; cool, fluffy, doll like, her cupid's bow mouth the latest shade, parted sufficiently to show two perfect front teeth, no more.

'Good morning Mr Andrews, is this your day?'

'No.'

'Oh! Is Mr Sandman expecting you?'

'No, but I must see him, it's really very urgent! Most urgent!'

'Come in.'

I stepped inside the door.

'I'll see if he can spare a minute.'

'Thank you.'

She closed the door behind me first looking up and down the street, I don't know why, maybe to make sure it was still there. Then, showing four front teeth, she motioned me towards the waiting room before tapping at the double doors and disappearing into the inner room that was the psychiatrist's holy of holies.

I didn't go into the waiting room. I didn't want to look at twelve month's old *Vogue* or *House and Garden*. I stood in the hall, trembling, fiddling with the brim of my hat. She seemed to be gone a long time. I looked at my wrist and frowned – no watch. Now that really was a stupid thing to do. Where could I possibly have left it? Never in my whole life had I forgotten to put on my watch, that is not since I was old enough to have one, and for a few occasions when I took it off... Her voice broke the silence.

'Please go in Mr Andrews.'

I nodded my thanks and passed her; still smiling. She closed the door after me. Sandman stood up behind his desk.

'Good morning, Mr Andrews, this is a surprise.'

'You've got to change it!'

It had slipped out. Slipped out? No, I had blurted it out like a small boy angrily accusing: vehemently; too loudly for this quiet room.

'You've got to change it,' I whispered as though to make up for my belligerence.

'Sit down, Mr Andrews.' His open hand indicated the chair opposite him. His voice was almost as quiet as his room. I sat.

'Now then, what seems to be the trouble?'

'Doctor, please, you must help me!'

'But that's what I am trying to do.'

'Yes I know, but you must help me now! NOW!'

'Please, Mr Andrews, gently... control yourself. Now just relax for a moment, take a few deep breaths and then tell me all about it. That's better. Yes?'

'It's the dream.' He nodded. 'I can't dream it anymore.'

'You mean you can't? Or you don't want to?'

'I don't want to. It's becoming too real... too lifelike.'

He smiled. 'You dreamed it last night?'

'Of course! I dream it every night.'

'Hmn-hmn, but that is exactly what you are meant to do.'

'Yes, yes I know, I know that, but it's... it's...' I couldn't seem to get the words out. I couldn't concentrate. I fumbled in my pockets for my cigarettes. He leaned across the desk shaking his head.

'Now, Mr Andrews, you know the theory behind this type of therapy. I explained it all to you. You were willing to undergo this treatment and you must see it through to the end or it will all have been a waste of time.'

'I can't!'

'Would you rather commit murder?'

'Commit murder?' I was shouting again. 'Commit murder! I do it every night, seven nights a week and each time it becomes more real, more horrible! Every detail is imprinted on my mind when I wake!'

'Good, good,' he murmured, 'we're making progress.'

'To what? When will it end?'

'It will end when we have discovered just whom it is you really want to kill and you no longer dream the dream.'

"How can he sit there like that and discuss it all so calmly? How can he sit there like that and smile? So safe, so smug, so secure. What would he do if I picked up that marble inkwell and hurled it at his sleek grey head? What would he do if I picked up that paper knife and thrust it between his ribs? Would he fight? Would he scream? Would I see the terror on his face? My own reflected in his eyes?"

He was watching me closely. Could he read my mind? He picked up the paper knife and twirled it between his fingers and then very deliberately placed it on the blotter in front of him.

'Perhaps,' he continued, 'it's your father you want to punish.'

'My father is dead; you know that.'

'Then perhaps it is his memory you are trying to kill. Or, maybe, it is yourself. We have to find out.'

'Why can't it be her?'

'Because the mind is far too fond of disguises. If it were her then you would transfer it to someone else, me for instance.'

'And when we have discovered who it is?'

'Then we must find out why. We must bring it out into the cold light of reason, turn it over, examine it, dissect it, and see it for what it is.'

He was obviously not going to be persuaded, I would have to try another tack.

'But if you succeed in curing me,' I said, 'what happens if you can't change the dream?'

'Now don't worry about that.' He drumbeat the paper knife on the desk for a moment. 'The mind, Mr Andrews, is like an orchard under irrigation, and the water with which it is irrigated are ideas, impressions, experiences. If the same idea keeps running down the same channel it digs deeper and deeper. This results in the formation of habit. Now we have formed under artificial stimulus of a certain part of your brain the habit of dreaming a particular dream. We have done this so that in your sleep you may harmlessly work out your compulsive behaviour.'

I nodded. All this had been explained to me before and he was only trying to reassure me.

'When we have unearthed the reason for this compulsive behaviour and have cured you, we dam up the channel through which this idea has been flowing and the dream stops. Now please, trust me, have faith and all will be well.'

'It might be too late.'

He shook his head slowly. 'I don't think so,' he said.

I sat still a moment wishing I could believe him, wishing I could have faith in him, the way he seemed to have himself. Perhaps my fears were groundless after all. He knew what he was doing and I had placed myself entirely in his hands.

'All right,' I said and took up my hat to leave.

'Before you go, maybe you would like to tell me about last night's dream so that we can find out just why it has terrified you so much.'

I put down my hat, placed my elbows on the desk and interlocking my fingers concentrated on my hands. I needed something to focus on.

'Well, I dreamed I woke up in the night, it was still dark, too dark to see what time it was. I switched on the bedside light and looked at my watch, it was four o'clock. My wife was lying next to me, still asleep. She looked very pretty. She is you know.' He nodded. 'She's very attractive my wife, a lovely woman. Well, suddenly I felt this urge and… and I couldn't help myself. I took up my pillow and brought it down over her face, slowly so as not to waken her. But she must have sensed what I was doing because suddenly she was wide awake: staring at me; but before

27

she could scream I brought the pillow down, down hard. She struggled and we rolled off the bed. She escaped and ran into the bathroom but before she could close the door I was after her. There was no escape. She screamed and fell backwards against the bath and... and the...'

'Go on.'

'And then I killed her. When she had stopped struggling I went to the bedroom, closed the bathroom door behind me, got dressed, went downstairs and made myself a cup of coffee. I don't remember any more.'

He sat a moment, thinking.

'But, Mr Andrews, this is almost an exact replica of what you have dreamed before. I cannot see why it...'

The relief I had experienced in relating my dream vanished in a wave of anxiety. I thudded the desk with the sides of my hands. 'There's something I should remember,' I said. 'There's something I have forgotten! Something terribly important but I have forgotten it!'

'I think you ought to take the day off,' he said softly. 'Take a walk. Go to the park. Spend a nice peaceful day doing nothing. Or better still go home and take your wife out. I'm sure she would appreciate a day off, hmn?' He smiled reassuringly and pressed the bell on his desk. 'And I'll see you on Wednesday for our next session. Now, if you don't mind, I have a patient waiting.'

I took up my hat and left. His next patient was a young woman. For some reason she reminded me of my wife and I smiled at her but she didn't return the smile.

She was waiting in the hall to usher me out; cool, fluffy and doll like. She looked up and down the street before closing the door behind me.

I decided to take a cab home, stopping on my way to buy a bunch of flowers for my wife. The traffic was pretty dense at that hour of the morning and as we neared our street I paid the cabby and walked the last hundred yards or so. There seemed to be a great deal of activity in our street.

'Stand back there! Stand back there!' A small crowd made reluctant way for an ambulance that clanged up the street. Quickening my step I broke into a run and dashed up the steps to our front door.

A uniform barred the way.

'One moment, sir.'

'I live here!' I shouted.

"Oh!" He looked at me from either side of his helmet's peak and then, taking me gently by the arm, led me into my own hall and up to two gentlemen who were talking quietly in a corner. They turned to look at us. The man holding my arm inclined his head in my direction and the first of the two gentlemen spoke.

'Mr Andrews?' I nodded. 'We have been trying to contact you all morning, at your office.'

'I wasn't there,' I said.

'Obviously.'

'What has happened? What are you doing in my house?' I couldn't think. The questions seemed childlike. It seemed a child's voice that asked them, not my voice, as though I was not really with them, as though I were dreaming.

'Have you seen this before?'

"Oh!" I said, sounding pleased, 'My watch.' I took it from the handkerchief in which it had been lying and inspected the broken strap, I was about to get a new one anyway, a gold bracelet if it didn't look too flashy.'

'Where did you find it?' I asked.

'In your wife's hand, Mr Andrews.'

And then I remembered.

*Antjie Somers*

*O*nce upon a time there was a village where nothing ever happened. Simple Stephan, who was a penny short of a shilling, sat in the sun all day at the back door and Red Rufus, the village smith, had so little work that he would every once and a while take his exercise on the one grey donkey that had quietly stood for years by the village pond.

But the sleepy hamlet was set astir when the handsome young farm boy, Peter, fell in love with the beautiful Marie, whose godfather, old Uncle Andres, promised the young couple a piece of his land in the valley... and the village clerk dusted down the marriage register in preparation for the wonderful day.

But then a very strange thing happened. Peter, so much in love that he could not sleep, wandered about in the moonlight one summer night and, deeply troubled by his love, he lay down in a hay meadow from where he could see Marie's house, and there, his gaze fixed on her window, he fell asleep.

The night was very still. Suddenly a bent ugly figure crept stealthily towards the meadow... Antjie Somers, the old witch who could sense from afar the beauties and the loves of men. She hobbled towards the sleeping youth and, bending over him, she fell violently in love when she saw how strong and handsome he was. Crooked and hideous she danced a magic dance with which to get Peter in her power and, when he wakened, she danced even more seductively to show him her love. But Peter, repelled by the crone's antics, leapt to his feet and ran away. Faster and faster he ran while the witch ran dancing after him. Her efforts all in vain, Antjie Somers grew suddenly purple with rage and in a moment transformed the boy into a crippled idiot, ten times uglier than Simple Stefan. The moon dropped beneath the horizon as Antjie Somers slunk panting away into the black night.

Peter sank to the ground in a weary, stupefied slumber while the eastern sky grew light.

The sun was well into the morning sky when uncle Andres, returning from the fields where he pastured his cattle, stumbled across Peter in the meadow. Horrified, he gathered together the village who stood aghast at the sight before them.

The last to arrive was poor Marie, who turned deathly pale, not knowing whether to scream, or run, or fall in a heap beside her lover.

No one could decide what had happened to bring about this hideous transformation until Simple Stefan, who was ugly and understood many things, suddenly stammered, 'It is the work of Antjie Somers!'

And perhaps, because he knew the pain of being ugly, he was the first to think of the means to help Peter.

'As soon as it is dark, Antjie Somers will return,' he told the gathered villagers, 'but I have heard that if she falls asleep before day breaks her powers will be broken.'

'Yes! Yes! If only we can make her sleep before daybreak!' Shouted the others. Then they put their heads together. Red Rufus said he would use his hammer. The village clerk suggested they drug her with cheap wine and Uncle Andres suggested a large beefsteak dosed with wolf poison. Finally it was agreed they would hold a barbecue in the meadow with plenty to eat and drink, music and dancing, and when Antjie Somers came sniffing up, they would charitably invite her to join them in feasting. They would then take it in turns to dance with her until exhausted she fell to the ground in a stupor. For no man alone could hope to outwit Antjie Somers.

The plan went well. As soon as she scented the merrymaking, the old hag could not resist the wine, the smell of the steaks and delicacies and, as the music grew wilder and wilder, she felt an irresistible urge to dance.

The clerk was the first to bow deeply before her and to dance stiff legged because it was not something he was used to but he did his best.

Then wild Uncle Andres grasped her around the waist and whirled her about.

Then round and round she went with Simple Stefan.

And then Red Rufus threw his mighty arms about her.

And even Peter, wakened by the din, danced with the old witch.

Everyone danced with Antjie Somers, ignoring her protests, until finally dead drunk and completely exhausted she fell like a bad pumpkin senseless to the ground and snored disgustingly.

At once Peter became his old handsome self. Marie, crying with joy, fell into his arms while the whole village danced about them singing, 'We snuffed out Antjie Somers with a dance!'

The next morning Antjie Somers had disappeared and was never heard of again, and after the wedding of Peter and Marie, the little village returned once more to its old sleepy ways and they lived happily ever after. That, anyway, is the legend.

# Pioneer

$\mathcal{I}$n these days of the affluent consumer society, of featherbedding and comfort, when we seem to spend so much of our time trying to ensure against pain and the hard knocks of life, it seems strange to reflect that just over a hundred years ago or so, on a dark night and in a violent sub-tropical storm, a youth on horseback crossed the raging torrent of an African river in flood to win the hand of the girl he loved. And, later in his life, when his thumb was injured in a hunting accident and obstinately refused to heal, he placed his hand on a rock and amputated the thumb with his penknife. In old age, while in Switzerland in exile from his beloved land, he extracted an offending tooth with the help of that same penknife. The man was Paul Kruger, known affectionately by his people as Oom Paul–Uncle Paul–and his was the true spirit of the pioneer. There were many like him: in America, Africa, Australia; wherever a man was prepared to stand on his own two feet and say in his heart–"Whatever comes, I am prepared to face it."

Sixty odd years ago in South Africa this spirit was personified for me in someone I will never forget. Her name was Betty Nel and, like myself at that time, she was a farmer, my nearest neighbour in fact. My family had just purchased a smallholding; sixty beautiful acres of Natal called Blue Hills where, for most of the time, I would be alone. A few days after I had moved in, a dirty, brown, battered old Chevrolet rattled up to stop in front of my verandah and a large, friendly looking woman climbed out of the car waving a paw a lumberjack would have been proud of. Within minutes of introducing herself, she made it quite clear she stood no nonsense from man or beast, especially man, and as long as I played straight with her, that was fine. But the good Lord help me if I turned out to be anything but honest. Was there anything I wanted? Could she be of help in any way? If I needed anything I had only to let her know. That was all she had come for, to make me welcome. I thanked her, genuinely appreciative of her kindness and, for a while, we sat on the stoep drinking coffee and talking before she had to go. Walking back to her car I noticed she moved with a decided roll to one side and, standing back to open the door for her, I glanced down. Her left leg from knee to ankle was an ugly twisted skein of livid scars.

For all her straight talk and down-to-earth-manner, Betty Nel was a shy woman, and a proud one. She had carved out her farm from virgin land. The house she lived in she had built herself, surrounded by outhouses and fences, roads and fertile fields that were all of her own making. When disaster struck, as it can do on South African farms, swiftly and often, she faced it alone and usually overcame. Once when her small herd of grade dairy cattle was threatened with extinction by East Coast fever, she moved into the cowshed to nurse them twenty-four hours a day and pulled most of them through, almost a miracle with this dreaded disease.

So independent was Betty Nel she even took a course in mechanics at a cousin's garage so she could repair all the farm machinery herself and not have to call in a man to do it for her–and this was a long time before women's lib. It was also the cause of her disfigurement and it was not until we had become very close friends that I dared to ask her for the story. At first she seemed reluctant to tell me. But Betty had inherited another quality from her pioneer forebears: another that, with the advent of mass communication, was also threatened; the ability to talk, to spin a good yarn or tell of an adventure. Or, as in this instance, to vividly recall an experience–if one might be pardoned the pun–a harrowing experience.

Although she pitched into anything and everything to do with running a mixed farm I never saw Betty in anything but women's dress. Not for her the more practical slacks and gumboots. On a typical African day of brilliant blue cloudless skies and a heat haze lying over the countryside, she sat on the hard metal seat of her tractor singing happily to herself, turning every now and again to make sure the harrow behind was behaving as it should. On a fairly steep hillside she had been at it since sun up and it was now well passed lunchtime. She was about to stop operations to eat when the tractor suddenly snorted, coughed, and stopped dead of its own accord. Betty climbed down and checked the obvious; fuel, carburettor, plugs and, unable to trace a fault, she decided to postpone lunch until the tractor was repaired. So, spanner in hand, she crawled underneath to see where the fault lay. The tractor suddenly lurched forward and Betty rolled sideways, a fraction too late. Her dress caught beneath the machine and, by the time she managed to get free, her leg was a bloody mess, her calf muscles severed below the knee and virtually ripped from the bone almost to her ankle. Had she not held them up as she hobbled painfully to her car parked close by, they would have dragged along the ground behind her. Climbing into the driver's seat, she had already torn enough skirt to form a crude bandage, she started the motor and set off. A short distance from her farm there was a trading store owned by an Indian couple who took one look at Betty's leg, the blood now practically reaching the running board and the man raced her into Pietermaritzburg and emergency where she was laid out on an operating table and about to be anaesthetised when she asked the surgeon what he intended to do. When told that the leg had to be amputated, Betty sat up and, refusing the anaesthetic in case something was done while she was unconscious, she watched as the muscles were sewn back on and the leg was saved.

Another of her stories concerned a hitchhiker she picked up and who, after a moment's driving pulled out a gun and ordered her to stop. Calmly she reached into the door pocket, pulled out her own gun and balancing it across her steering arm said, 'Who shoots first?' and slammed on the brakes. The man fled.

Betty Nel, that wonderful woman, battered to death during a robbery was found in the boot of that selfsame car. I still sometimes think of her.

# Another Christmas Carol

*Y*ou may very well think this to be a tall tale from *Ripley's Believe It Or Not* and I would sympathise with you wholeheartedly as, for myself, I still find it difficult, almost impossible, to believe, but there are more things in heaven and earth than are dreamt of as a certain Mister William Shakespeare once said.

It was a dark and stormy night. Isn't that the most famous opening line in fiction? I had just enough small change to pay for a coffee from the hotdog stand across the street (I could have done with a hotdog as well, with lashings of mustard, but my finances didn't stretch to that) and had laid my cardboard down in the shelter of a deeply recessed shop doorway when he appeared, seemingly out of nowhere, because the street had been quite deserted a moment before and only the attendant stood at the hotdog stall, waiting for custom.

He eased himself down opposite me onto the cold concrete, obviously never having learnt, or so I thought, that a good sheet of cardboard and newspaper are excellent as insulation against the cold, and introduced himself quite politely.

'Good evening,' he said. 'I am God.'

He could see my raised eyebrows over the rim of the polystyrene cup I was holding, warming my hands a little and the steam from the coffee warming my nostrils a lot. "Oh, Lord!" I thought. "We've got a right one here."

'Jesus!' Was what I said out loud.

'No, no, that was two thousand and odd years ago,' was his response. 'After that little debacle I returned to being just me.'

I pondered this for a moment, took a sip of coffee, almost scalding my tongue, and held out the cup in his direction.

'Playing the Good Samaritan are we?' There was just the hint of a smile.

Was there also just the hint of a sneer accompanying that remark, that smile? "Suit yourself," I thought and withdrew the offer.

'So, God,' I said, feeling just the faintest bit foolish at addressing a down and out as the Almighty but feeling I had best humour him, 'what is it you're doing sitting in a shop doorway on a dark and stormy night with another down and out and refusing, I may add, to accept his hospitality?'

'Talking to him,' he said.

'That sounds logical,' I pursed my lips and nodded in acquiescence.

'Did you know Thomas Aquinas tried to prove my existence by means of logic?'

'Did he now?' I said this with amazement in my voice. 'No, I never knew that.'

'Failed dismally of course,'

'Of course.'

There was silence for a while. Either he had, for the moment, given up the idea of being God or he was gazing into the middle distance seeking inspiration.

'I take it ... ' I felt I had to choose my words carefully here. I am a pacifist at heart, well a total coward if the truth were known, and I wouldn't have liked it if this madman was to suddenly up and lunge at me. For all I knew he had a weapon secreted somewhere about his person, probably a flick-knife... 'I take it you are flesh and blood.'

'No. Like I said, that was two thousand and odd years ago.'

I resisted the temptation to stretch out my hand or give him a good kick to affirm the solidity or otherwise of his corporeal existence. I couldn't see through him to the shop window behind so I presumed he was lying through his teeth. He was as corporeal as I am. Though how come, considering the lightness of the summery type garb he wore, he wasn't shivering fit to bust or turning blue with the cold? How come his teeth weren't chattering and his knees knocking together as his legs trembled? I gave an involuntary shiver and reached in the pocket of my raggedy greatcoat for the hip flask size bottle of scotch I kept there, only for emergencies you understand. I unscrewed the cap and, even though he had refused my offer of coffee, I thought as a gentleman of the road he would accept a swig of the old brew but, to my astonishment, he declined with a shake of his head so I went ahead and took a good hard slug as he watched.

'Do you think that was a good invention of mine?' He asked.

'What?' I gasped when I had more or less got my breath back and the wheezing lessened.

'Alcohol.'

'We...ell... yes... and... no. It has its pros and cons if you get my meaning.'

'In other words it was a mistake.'

'No-o, I didn't say that. Now don't you start putting words in my mouth.'

'Hmn...'

He sat ruminating for a while. A couple of times he opened his mouth as if to say something but closed it again before anything other than a cloud of steam came out with his breath. This made me think again of his corporeal existence. A supernatural being like God would not necessarily have breath, least of all with steam in it, not like a flesh and blood animal such as we are. Eventually, as it turned out, he decided on a means of continuing the debate by saying, 'You asked the reason for my being here. Well, I thought I'd mosey along and find out how... '

Here he stopped and let off more steam before continuing with, 'I tell you what, as one of my creations, why don't you ...? What's your name by the way?

"Aha!" I thought. "Gotcha! If you're God and you know everything there is to know, you wouldn't have to ask me that. You would be able to tell me."

'John, isn't it?'

Amazement on my eyebrow sat, as Shakespeare would have said. I took another slug of whisky.

'How did you know that?' I squeaked as if I had taken a lung full of helium.

'Well, John, as you are fully aware, I have the reputation of knowing everything. I am after all, Alpha and Omega. Your name is John and when in three years four months and two days time at exactly eleven thirty of the p.m. you die in the gutter of cirrhosis of the liver and various other nasty ailments, all your own fault you understand, nothing to do with me, nothing whatsoever, you will be collected in a body bag and a label will be affixed to your big toe with John Doe written on it as you are carted off to the city morgue to be buried in an unmarked grave. Got the picture?'

I nodded, open-mouthed. To say I was speechless would be too obvious for words. I wondered he didn't mention the seconds.

'So, John, come to my assistance and tell me where I went wrong? Inform me of my various mistakes. Put me on the right track as it were.'

I have to confess at this point, in the words of any writer of consequence recording these details, I gulped quite hard. God expected me to criticise him and all his works? Come off it. A lightning bolt could zap down at any moment burning me to a crisp and sending shards of plate glass flying in all directions. I could even be decapitated. I decided on delaying tactics by changing the conversation.

'Tell me,' I said, 'as a matter of interest, do angels have... ?'
Here I stopped.

'Ye-es?' He smiled again, somewhat indulgently this time.

'Do angels have...?

'Well, come on, John. Spit it out, man. No need to be shy. After all I did invent it.'

'Yes, well... '

'By your hesitation I must presume you consider it to be one of my mistakes. Now why would that be, hmn? Elucidate.'

'You're putting words in my mouth again. I was only going to ask, do angels have sex?'

'How did I know that would be the very first question you would ask? Why on earth, I mean why in heaven, would angels want to have sex?'

'Fun?'

'Fun? Fun! They spend their eternity worshipping and adoring me, what more fun could they possibly ask for?'

'None I suppose, if you put it that way.'

'That's the way I put it. And why would you suggest sex is one of my mistakes? Did you never enjoy having it?'

'We... ell, yes... yes of course I did, when I was a young lusty lad full of life's promise.'

'And sperm.'

'And what? Oh, yes ... and that. And of course your injunction to go forth and multiply.'

He seemed to ponder on this for a while and then frowning mightily and in a slow drawl, said, 'Yes, now that was definitely a mistake. Had I realised in the beginning, while there was still dark upon the waters, just how passionately you lot would embrace it and how potent my invention was I might have diluted it somewhat. As it is, and has always been, you're worse than rabbits and only I know how bad they are. Breed breed breed as though this planet can support all the breeding you're capable of despite the various little stratagems I've put in the way to try and slow you all down.'

'Such as.'

'STD's? Imaginative diversions, deviations, aberrations and perversions? Various plagues and other diseases when considered necessary to reduce the population, but that was in bygone days before you cottoned on and increased your medical knowledge so undoing a great deal of my good work. Why did I bother? After all I gave you free will and if you want to overpopulate your planet so be it. No more will I stick my oar in as the saying goes. Fortunately I've never had to bother myself too much with wars, ethnic cleansing, that sort of thing, as you're all too eager to have a go and you're fairly good at that. But tell me, what went wrong with you personally? You and sex I mean.'

'Infidelity, jealousy, heartbreak, harrowing tears, sleepless nights, anxiety, neurosis, in some cases psychosis and finally impotence. It's been a long long time.'

'All good things come to an end or they wouldn't be all good things.'

'And it's messy.' He was not going to get the better of me. I was going to have the last of this little exchange.

'Messy?'

'Body fluids, bodily functions, stuff like that. Smelly and messy and painful, very painful, for the woman that is, giving birth. Very painful. Very messy.'

'Yes, well I am supposed to have put the onus for that on the mother of you all when I kicked those two reprobates out of the Garden of Eden. They shouldn't have started the ball, or balls, rolling in the first place.' Here he gave a little chuckle.

'You mean it really existed? The Garden of Eden?'

'Of course it didn't. It's a myth. Don't you know what a myth is?'

'A lady with a lisp?' God frowned. 'Only joking. Anyway I am totally relieved to hear from your very own lips that that story is definitely a myth otherwise we would all be descendent from an act of incest and that is not a thought worth thinking about.'

'You're dead to rights on that one, John boy, but myths can be jolly useful for pulling the wool over gullible people's eyes. So tell me, what's the alternative to copulation? The stork? The gooseberry bush? Any bright ideas?'

'Not really.' I shrugged.

'Well, I hate to admit this but I'm afraid I do tend to agree with you that sex was a humongous blunder on my part. Oh, not for the reasons you've come up with but because, rather than rejoice in the gift I have given them, it has caused all sorts of rather nasty people with the most horrendous personal problems, inhibitions and repressions to believe they have a reason, an excuse rather, to make life hell on earth for others, and all in my name naturally. But this is beginning to depress me. Let's move on to another topic shall we?'

I really didn't know what topic to move on to so, in the lacuna created by God's depression, I took a half-smoked butt from my breast pocket and proceeded to light it with my last remaining match. He watched dolefully as I took a good lung full and exhaled with lips like a chimpanzee. A cigarette really goes well with a cup of coffee, especially that first drag.

'To that aforementioned cirrhosis,' he said, 'add emphysema.'

I smiled. 'It's not the cough that carries you off it's the coffin they carry you off in.'

He didn't seem to find that amusing.

'Well... ' I mused, being philosophical and that, 'we all have to go sometime to that bourn from which no traveller returns as Shakespeare had it, except that there was Hamlet on the battlements at Elsinore on a dark and stormy night... '

'Elsinore doesn't have battlements.'

'According to Willy it has and there he is, Hamlet, faced with his poor old dad who has returned against all the odds from that very same bourn to fill Hamlet in with his tale of woe. Still, even the greatest of playwrights can make the occasional booboo, can they not? And you did it didn't you?'

'I was never a playwright.'

'No, I meant, you came back, after three days, and showed yourself to all and sundry, and there was old doubting Thomas wouldn't believe it until he'd stuck a grubby finger in your side. Must've given him quite a turn.'

'Of all the hare-brained schemes I ever dreamed up it was ridiculous that I even thought of it in the first place. This was the one that had absolutely no chance of working, not in a month of Sundays, or Saturdays, or Fridays. Hey, John! You could belong to all three religions and give yourself long weekends. And why not? In the end they're all supposed to point in my direction. Chance would be a fine thing,' he added, a tinge of bitterness in his voice. 'Not only are they constantly at each other's throats, they're constantly at throats within their own lot. And again they keep on and on about it all being in my name. You see now, why I consider it a total failure.'

'Not really.'

'Meaning you don't see or not a total failure?'

'I don't see.'

'Well let me give you the whole low-down, from the very beginning.'

'Genesis?'

'No, not Genesis. Forget all that. I should never have given those ancients carte blanche to write all that stuff. In the first place none of them had taken a creative writing course such as you can get nowadays at any good university. In the second place they were all human, warts and all, aches and pains, good opinions and bad, pride and prejudices, sense and nonsense, hang-ups and hang-downs but, whatever entered their heads it was, of course, written down as holy writ, altogether now, ta-ra!... in my name! And the things they said about me! How I am a jealous god, am angry, vindictive, vengeful, absolutely frightening in fact.'

'Well you did come up with some rather strange, one might even say, macabre manifestations.'

'For example.'

'Sending Moses up the mountain to collect the commandments and keeping him there an inordinate length of time knowing full well that the minute his back was turned the hoi polloi down below would get up to mischief. Ever heard of the cat and the mice? I mean, what was the point of that?'

'I was testing them.'

'Seems to me in those days you did an awful lot of testing. What about Abraham being told to sacrifice his son? What was that all about? Testing again?'

He shrugged. 'I stopped him from actually doing it, didn't I? It was more of a practical joke really.'

'A what?!' I could hardly believe my ears. 'If that's the case all the things they said about you are true. Talk about a twisted sense of humour. And what about Job? Same thing? Jonah? Hmn?'

'I did do some good things as well you know but we're getting away from what I was going to tell you.'

'Oh, fire away, but it's getting awfully late and I'm beginning to grow sleepy. The rosy-fingered dawn ... ' He cut me off sharpish.

'All right already! I'll be brief. Well, nobody ever seemed to take any notice of what I told them. For example, having put to the torch and laid waste the cities of the plain I then had to turn Lot's missus into a pillar of salt for disobeying me and turning around for a look-see. I had expressly forbidden that.'

'Why?'

'Why?'

'Yes, Why?'

'Because I had. Do I need a reason?'

'I suppose not. Maybe you took as your precedent what happened previously in an earlier religion, Orpheus's girlfriend, Euridice was told not to look back and...'

'Please! Please don't bring up the Greek myths, or any other old pagan rubbish, but let's stick to the matter in hand or we'll be here all night.'

'I hate to point this out to you but I am here all night.'

'As I was saying, injunction by voice alone bellowing down from a mountain top being insufficient – you will notice it hasn't happened for a very long time – I decided I would have to make a personal appearance and, in order to do that, it would be necessary for me to become as one of you disobedient lot and this is where some of the trouble started. You personally, with your obviously extensive knowledge of theology, will no doubt be aware that Lucifer, most beautiful of the archangels, bringer of light, darling, curly headed (metaphorically speaking) boykin, was my firstborn and, in filial devotion, he offered to come down to earth and single-handed sort you all out but I had already decided I was going to do it myself. If you want something done well, do it yourself and, no, Shakespeare didn't say that. At least I don't think he did. What I didn't tell Lucifer unfortunately was that I was going to do it in disguise as my second born, Joshua, me actually being Joshua if you get my meaning. Clear so far?

Well, naturally Lucy, we called him that as a term of endearment you understand, it had no other connotation, was extremely disappointed. Disappointed? He threw a hissy fit, stamped his beautiful foot, and stormed off before I even had a chance to tell him, if that was the way he felt, to go to hell, and so the Bringer of Light became the Prince of Darkness.'

'Jealousy again.'

'Right.' He pointed a stiff index finger at me, thumb raised. 'In the meantime I scouted around for a suitable couple to parent me as it were and settled on Joseph and Mary which was kosher as it was among my chosen people – little did I realise what I was letting them in for as though they hadn't suffered enough, what with Pharaoh and all – but that is how I became Joshua bar Joseph. Jesus, as you are no doubt fully aware, is Greek but raising alleluias to Joshua doesn't sound quite so noble, poetic and holy does it now? It was round about this time of the year that I was actually born.'

'Yes, the decorations have been up for months. The big sell is getting so I wonder they even bother to take them down.'

'So what's the first thing that happens to celebrate my birth?'

'Three wise men come out of the east bearing wonderful gifts.'

'No. Herod orders the slaughter of all those poor little innocents hoping I would be among them. Great start. Anyway, Herod was too late and I grew up to fulfil my destiny, the purpose I had set myself. I gathered my disciples and I walked Judea and Galilee teaching, sometimes uplifting, sometimes gently reproving, sometimes letting off steam like that time in the temple… '

'Sometimes performing miracles.'

He looked at me as though I had said something extremely distasteful.

'Miracles?'

'Yes. You know, water into wine? That sort of thing.'

'Cheap parlour tricks. Any competent magician can do it.'

'Raising Lazarus from the dead.'

'Lazarus wasn't dead, he was suffering from narcolepsy.'

'Oh.'

'Anyway, to continue, it was hard work I can tell you, hell on the feet if nothing else, schlepping across burning deserts. It was bliss sometimes to wriggle one's toes in the Sea of Galilee. I mistimed it though, didn't I? I should have waited another two thousand and odd years. After all, what is time to me? If I had left it till now I could have had my own website and spread my word on the Internet. Would have saved a lot of agony. And what was all that agony in aid of? Did my sacrifice improve man's behaviour? Did it hell! If anything it's worse than ever. Man is still vicious, cruel, unprincipled, unenlightened, avaricious, murderous, deceitful, a lying conniving thieving tripe hound.'

'Okay! No more. I got the picture.'

'And that, my friend, is why I say it was a failure, a complete fiasco. Do you not agree?'

There was now a look of infinite sadness on his face and I was on the point of stretching out my hand to touch and comfort him when his attention was drawn to something happening across the street.

'Hello! What's happening there?'

I turned to look and saw a gaggle of young girls in mini-skirts, high heels, low-cut angora type sweaters and cheap jewellery, five or six, I don't remember exactly how many, around the hotdog stand. They had obviously ordered food because they spat their chewing gum out on the pavement and, hotdogs in hand, started eating, none too delicately I might add. I wondered if it reminded God of the loaves and fishes and had just decided not to mention it when things started to turn nasty. The hotdog man wanted payment. The girls obviously were not going to pay and it now became evident to me that they were every one as drunk as skunks. One of them hurled the remains of her hotdog in the young man's face and that started the riot as, with much unseemly and unmaidenly cursing and shrieking, like Bacchantes or Harpies they attacked the stall and the poor guy trying desperately to protect it. God got to his feet.'

'Where are you going?' I yelled in some alarm.

'To intervene,' he said.

'No! You mustn't do that. These days girls are even more feral than boys. They'll kill you!'

'No they won't. I'll reason with them.'

'After what you've just been saying, you'll try reasoning with them? Are you crazy?'

But he was already half way across the road. I took a swig of my whisky, polished it off in fact and hurriedly lay down, pulling my coat collar up well over my ears. I didn't want to know any more. Like I said before I am basically a coward, so I closed my eyes and went to sleep. I think later I heard sirens wailing but I couldn't be too sure about that.

When I opened my eyes again, it was early dawn. If there had been a cock around it would no doubt have crowed. I looked across the street. There was no sign that anything untoward had occurred, no sign of the hotdog stand, no girls, no God, nothing more than a bit of a mess in the road.

For some reason I kept on hearing a voice in my head, "This was my second coming," it said, "my second coming, my second coming."

Well, if that's the case, I thought, the world has missed it.

And, damn it, I forgot to ask him the sixty four thousand dollar question – who really wrote the works attributed to William Shakespeare?

# The Museum Mysteries

*P*ROLOGUE:
'Slowly, slowly, take care. Has it been photographed?'
'Of course.'

'Do you realise what this could be? This piece is almost unique. In the whole of Greece only two like it have ever been found. Remove that last little bit of earth there, next to his eye, and lift it clear.'

Vincenzo brushed away the last of the earth with a soft brush and was about to lift the object but his trembling hands and her obvious excitement at the discovery got the better of them.

'No, no! Let me do it,' she said.

'Careful! It's going to break.'

'Not this beauty. Not in my hands. Tender loving care is what it deserves and tender loving care is what it will get. Pass the tray,' she ordered as she lifted the cup from its resting place. They thought of it as a cup of some kind; it couldn't really be anything else despite its size. They knelt for a long while, one on either side, silently admiring their find, giving it another little light dusting with the brush. It gazed back at them with startlingly blue eyes as if it were newly modelled rather than lying buried beneath the accumulated detritus deposited over the millennia.

'It's perfect,' she whispered, almost in awe, as though if she spoke any louder the piece might shatter. Not that it appeared to be that fragile but you never know. 'Absolutely perfect. Not a mark, not a blemish, not a flaw, not a crack or a chip, just perfect, as if it were made yesterday rather than… how long ago? Two and half? Three thousand years?'

They remained for a long while kneeling in admiring silence as though entranced which, in a way, is what they were. It was almost as though it was impossible to move. Some of the others, sensing something momentous had happened and piqued with curiosity, stopped whatever they were doing and came over to take a look.

'Do you notice something strange about it?' she asked, not addressing anyone in particular.

'What?'

'The eyes are blue, the brightest blue. You would have thought they would have been brown, yes? But no, they're blue. The colour hasn't deteriorated in the least and it seems, the way they look at you, they could almost be alive, watching you.'

'Could it be like, you know, one of those paintings where the eyes seem to follow you if you move?' It was the youngest member of the team who put this forward and for a while there was silence as no one seemed inclined to answer her question. Then the silence was broken by a voice saying, 'It is beautiful. Congratulations, Professa, you are going to make archaeological history.'

'That's true,' somebody else chipped in, 'because we've found another one.'

*C*HAPTER 1
The almost inaudible soporific ticking of the large old station clock with its slightly chipped and stained enamel face, was the only sound to be heard until the old counter bell, so seldom used, broke the silence with a sudden strident ring that had him nearly jumping out of his skin. He was so used to the night's silence, he no longer heard the clock's steady ticking, each second ticking his life away, though if it stopped because someone had forgotten to wind it, then he immediately missed it.

Sergeant Antonio Modafferi, more than thirty years a police-man, never to rise above the rank of sergeant, and currently manning the desk in an otherwise totally deserted station; not even a prisoner to watch over, with whom to share a cup of coffee or keep occasional and congenial company with, looked up from the newspaper in which he had been so completely absorbed and, with an expression of some surprise, regarded the woman who seemed suddenly to have materialised out of nowhere on the far side of the counter. Until the ringing of the bell he hadn't heard a thing, not a door opening, or closing, no footsteps on the tiled floor, not a discreet cough, nothing, so engrossed had he been in the football results and the latest political shenanigans that seemed to eternally beset his native country.

The doings of the Mafia and politicians that continuously grab the headlines are always intriguing; and were they so very far apart he wondered? Politicians and crooks? Crooks and politicians? Who really knows? Someone as innocent, as naïve, as ill-informed as Antonio Modafferi certainly would have no idea. He had turned to the sports page and was pleased to see Reggino Calcio had won their last match by three goals to one. That was good news after two previous disasters. If they had carried on in that fashion it would have meant relegation for sure which would have been most unfair because they were in fact a very good side, just a little slap dash now and again, undisciplined, but what the hell, one can't be on tip-top form all the time and, anyway, isn't that very Italian? Everybody, even a footballer, is entitled to a bad day now and again and the team had recently suffered a couple of injuries that put two of their best players out of action for a while; that and a two game suspension for a really outrageous tackle that could easily have caused broken bones and a riot in the stands.

This hour of the night, that is this time in the early morning rather, the station was the best place to catch up with a person's reading. The tiny apartment he called home, a spitting distance from the station, the walk there and back on and off duty being his only daily exercise was out of the question. During the day there was never a moment's quiet, what with screaming brats all over the place like swarms of squealing mice, their shrill piercing voices enough to bring on a severe headache; mothers yelling at them and at each other, fathers yelling at mothers.

His wife of many years, Capricia, he equated with Shakespeare's shrew but who, seeing as to how he was in no sense a Petruchio, he had never managed to tame, was hooked on an endless diet of mindless television. In particular she liked watching those awful game shows, especially ones involving women being encouraged, no urged, to do, in his opinion, stupid demeaning things in front of a screaming audience and for all the country to see; all dignity and self restraint and sometimes even garments having been discarded. Not altogether of course but enough to titillate if you like that sort of thing. It was a wonder the various icons and statuettes of saints in the apartment, in particular Saint Agnes, patron saint of virgins among other things, hadn't turned their faces to the walls in total disgust. Have these women no shame? Antonio, it had to be admitted, was a bit on the prudish side and if he could have his way all this modern fascination with sex was extremely unhealthy and should be severely curtailed. It couldn't do any good. Modern fascination? On a more rational level he had to admit that fascination had been going on he supposed since cavemen roamed the world. Ancient Rome and Pompeii certainly indulged but he personally could do without it thank you very much and that was that, no more need be said.

He had momentarily put aside his book on Greek mythology which he was beginning to find quite heavy going, fascinating though it was, in order to scan the local newspaper and, when nothing more could grab his attention there, he would go back to his ancient gods and goddesses. He especially liked looking at the illustrations. In fact, before he picked up the newspaper, he had been reading about Selene, putting the book aside in what seemed only a minute past but must have been much longer. Antonio was quite sure his ancestors way back were Greek, this part of Italy and Sicily having once been virtually colonised by them. In fact there was still a region where the inhabitants spoke a dialect one could describe as Greetalian or a word to that effect, maybe there is a word for it, and as the old saying goes, same face, same race.

Mythology apart, the books Antonio enjoyed most were detective thrillers, in particular a series set in Venice, a city over which he held the most romantic visions and which he would like to visit one day even though he thought the reality might be a little different to his dreams. Isn't that always the way? It's the same as with people you hear talked about; when you meet them they're nothing like you had imagined. He thought this particular detective very true to life though, very down to earth, not glamorised in any way but a real human being, a real policeman, warts and all; a bit like himself really, partial to his pasta, maybe not intellectual but certainly intelligent, and Antonio was quite amazed to discover one day that the author was a lady. Not that ladies couldn't write excellent books and there were some who seemed to specialise in detective stories though they did seem to be few and far between. Hardly surprising he supposed. Did it all start with that famous English author, Agatha Christie whose books were a jolly good read but, in his opinion, absolute bunkum as far as police work was concerned? But then you never know really; England and the English are very different to Italy and the Italians and that could apply to police work so who was he to criticise? The Venetian detective on the other hand was so real he wondered if maybe the authoress wasn't married to one or, maybe, was even in the force herself. Many a time in his youth he had visions of himself capturing criminals in exciting car chases such as he saw in American movies, especially those ones in San Francisco where steep hills, sharp corners, and squealing tyres were involved, and at one time even thought of emigrating to the States so that his dreams could come true but instead he fell in love, got married and stayed put, and the reality in Maroccia, this little backwater of a town, hardly more than a village really, its inhabitants with a village mentality not so different now as a hundred or more years ago or even earlier, had been entirely different.

As far back as he could remember in this usually tranquil corner of the world nobody had ever entered the station at this time of night. In fact he was surprised the station had never been closed down and merged with one of the bigger towns in the area where there ware enough naughty goings - on to keep a person busy and make life interesting. This little town was usually blissfully and innocently asleep unless something like the croup kept a family awake, or an earth tremor, a seismic shock that, if it didn't actually shake them up, startled them wide-eyed with terror out of their beds.

In an hour or two the cocks would crow and it would be time for folk to get up and start another day, time to open shop, bake the bread, do the milking or go back to the fields for another day's labour. In a couple of hours Antonio Modafferi could make his way home to his own bed and try to sleep through the noise made by the squeaking mice and their loud mouthed parents. In the meantime, standing before him was this tiny strange birdlike creature with the obviously ruffled feathers who he hadn't heard come in, who seemed to have materialised out of nowhere, and who he now had to deal with. Her entrance in fact made him aware for the first time in years of the clock's steady ticking. It forced him to glance up at it. Was its sound magnified at that moment or was that just his imagination? Then he turned his attention back to his visitor.

'It's evil,' she said in a tone that made his blood curdle. It was not because he was squeamish where realities of flesh, blood, and guts are concerned. He had seen enough injury and death brought about by both natural and unnatural means; farm accidents, fights, shootings, stabbings, but there is another dimension he would rather not think about, although he didn't consider for one moment that, like those around him, he was in any way superstitious. No, but for his mother of blessed memory, one of the most devoted of church goers in the district who spent more hard-earned money on candles than was good for either her or the family – it's a wonder she didn't have calluses on her knees –

the very mention of the word 'evil' conjured up visions of fiery torments in hell for all eternity. She had wailed enough about it while still around to plant in her children the fear of damnation without respite. It was a wonder, he thought, that the gates of hell hadn't been locked against newcomers, there being such overcrowding and no more room down there.

Antonio had two brothers and two sisters and there were a couple of bambini who had died in infancy – he still visited and laid flowers on their graves together with mama's, praying that what she had prophesied whilst alive hadn't come true for her now she was dead. The bambini should be all right. They hadn't really had much time for sinning and they did depart this earthly vale with the church's blessing so maybe they spent a short time in purgatory before passing on to everlasting bliss. He remembered how each one had looked in his tiny coffin. Their waxen doll like images still gave him the shivers and for some reason they were currently brought vividly to mind as if their demise had been only yesterday.

So he regarded this strange looking woman with some apprehension. He had a bad feeling about her and it was not only because she was not exactly a sight for sore eyes. She was painfully thin, almost skeletal, with sunken cheeks and deep almost purple rings under her eyes; eyes that didn't seem to focus on anything in particular. In fact Antonio wondered if she were not looking at something above and beyond his head and was almost tempted to turn around and take a look, instead of which he shuddered, felt the hairs on his neck stand on end and regarded his visitor with growing unease. One blue veined bony hand was placed on her chest. The fingers weren't like claws or talons; rather they were like the slender fingers found on delicate porcelain statuettes of shepherds and shepherdesses, easily broken.

'Who's in charge here?' She finally gasped, having stood silent for a while except for the loud wheezing, in order to try and get back her breath. 'I need to speak with someone in charge.' She was wearing a plain black skirt and a flimsy silk blouse beneath which Antonio could swear he could see the rhythm of her heartbeat. There was no sign of any jewellery and she placed an old fashioned reticule on the counter which he eyed askance.

'And what may all this be about?' He responded softly with a quite reasonable question of his own when, after a moment, he found his voice.

It had to be something serious if for no other reason than she shouldn't be up and about fully dressed, no matter how inadequately, at this hour. To make matters worse she was a total stranger, someone he had never seen before and he knew everyone in the village and its surroundings. Where had she come from? Could she be visiting someone he knew? Why did she choose to come to this particular police station?

She had started to struggle for breath again, her mouth falling open and a tiny rivulet of saliva descending from one corner onto her chin. She wiped it away with the back of a hand. 'I need to speak to someone in charge.' The words came out staccato one by one. Now he could hear her desperate wheezing and wondered if she was going to drop dead right there and then. He felt a sudden pang of sympathy. Surely if she did she was going to suffer all of hell's torments just as his mother foretold and it was his duty, not only as a policeman but as a good Catholic, to render immediate assistance. Who should he call first? His chief? A doctor? Or the local priest?

Father Benedict was old and not prone to washing too often, either his clothes or himself, particularly in the winter. He was also hard of hearing and felt the telephone ring by the vibrations next to his bed rather than hearing the sound of the bell. Also he resented getting up in the middle of the night. His resentment went as far back as the seminary when he was forced to get up in the middle of the night for Vigil. So Antonio decided there wasn't much point in sending for Father Benedict. By the time he arrived at the station, if he arrived at all, the woman would more than likely be beyond spiritual aid.

'If you would like to take a seat over there...' Antonio pointed to the odd assortment of rickety chairs the otherwise empty station had acquired sometime in the distant past... 'I'll see what I can do.' He still wasn't too sure about whom he should call but finally, as he watched her pick up her reticule and shuffle away, decided to call his chief, hoping he would be at home; but then why shouldn't he be at four in the morning?

It seemed to take an eternity to get through on the telephone but finally the receiver at the other end was lifted from its cradle and a husky, obviously none too pleased, sleepy voice growled, 'Yes?'

'Chief,' Antonio said, somewhat more light-hearted than he intended but the relief that he had got someone to talk to got the better of him. 'This is Sergeant Modafferi here.'

'I know who it is. What other idiot would think of calling me at this... hold on a minute...' There was a pause while a light was being switched on so that Chief Inspector Greco could put on his reading glasses or squint at his bedside clock and ascertain the time... 'ungodly hour! What the hell do you want?'

'I er... I seem... that is... I... well I seem to have a bit of a problem here.'

'Is that so? You're a policeman, solve it.'

'Not that easy.' He said this very quickly in case the chief was about to put down the phone.

'Okay okay, so what's the problem? Give it to me fast so I can get back to sleep.'

'I have a woman here clutching her chest in pain.'

'Then send for an ambulance and stop disturbing my rest.'

'She said, well rather insisted actually, she needed to talk to someone in charge.'

'Well, aren't you supposed to be in charge? What are you doing there if you're not in charge? Get on with it. Find out what she wants and then get rid of her. All right, dear.'

'What?'

'What?'

'You called me dear.'

'Don't talk rubbish.'

'I heard you. You quite distinctly called me dear.'

'Idiot. I was talking to my wife who would like to go back to sleep as well so get on with it and don't bother me again. Ring headquarters and ask to speak to Inspector Giuseppe Borelli. Tell him I personally want him to take charge of this case.' The line went dead. Antonio could imagine what the chief was saying before he tried to go back to sleep and was glad he wasn't there to hear it. He looked at the phone in his hand, depressed and lifted the cradle, dialled again and waited.

The woman now looked in a very bad way indeed, she had returned to lean heavily on the counter, virtually on the point of expiring Antonio thought, his forebodings increased tenfold.

'Would you like a glass of water?' He asked but before she could answer, a voice as growling as the first came on the line.

'Yes?'

'Good morning.'

'Oh, piss off will you? What's good about it?'

'This is desk Sergeant Modafferi at the Maroccia station.'

'I know who it is.'

'I have a slight situation here which needs your urgent attention.' He thought he sounded a bit more in control, more business like, than with his first call.

'If it's a slight problem why should it need my urgent attention? In fact for that matter why should it need anybody's urgent attention? Go away. Sort it out yourself.'

'I have spoken with the chief inspector and he wants you personally to take charge of this case.'

'I bet the bastard does,' Borelli growled. 'Okay give me half an hour.' And the line went dead.

Borelli, who hadn't done so before, now switched on his bedside light and lay looking at the ceiling. He wondered if he should take a shower but decided it was a bit early for that so scratched himself quite vigorously, following the scratch wherever it moved until, satisfied there would be no more itch, he threw back the bedclothes and got out of bed to look for his trousers. He hadn't expected to be starting his day this early and wondered if he had a clean pair of socks he schlepped his way across to his ancient much battered chest of drawers, he loved the feel of the carpet pile under his bare feet, and a clean shirt maybe? Oh, hell! He might as well take that shower after all, what's another ten fifteen minutes?

****

'It's evil! Evil I tell you… here… Oh, God! The pain, the pain in my chest.' She could hardly gasp it out but the sceptical Giuseppe Borelli who had a deal of experience with the weird and wonderful in human nature believed somehow she was faking it; but, if so, the question was why should she do that? What did she hope to gain by it? What was she doing in the police station in the first place?

'What is evil?' he sighed, never taking his eyes off her, studying her now rather in the manner of someone examining a specimen of some kind.

She glared at him across the counter her hand still held over her heart. Her eyes seemed suddenly to have come into focus.

'Here... here... here.' It was almost a case of mia culpa as she thumped her bony chest.

'All right, madam, please, calm down.' Borelli said, showing her both palms, fingers pointed towards the ceiling as though he was figuratively pushing her away, even though he knew the gesture to be totally ineffectual. 'Someone else is coming to see to you and we have called the doctor so he shouldn't be long in coming.' This was a downright lie but he thought it might soothe her, calm her down a little. 'If you're in pain what you need,' he continued, 'is not a police station but a hospital, no?'

'No!' she shrieked. 'No no no! I don't want a doctor! You're not listening to me! Why won't you listen to me?'

"Perhaps it should be an asylum rather than a hospital," he thought. "Why do I always get them?" He went on to wonder, but then he already knew the answer. Ever since he had regrettably and unintentionally made the chief inspector look an idiot on a television chat show he had been assigned every crackpot case that came into the Critone station and this was probably the worst making him trail all the way out to the sticks. He really had no idea what to expect next from this obviously deranged woman.

He smiled at the memory of what had happened on that programme. It wasn't too difficult to make the chief look like an idiot; as far as he was concerned the man *was* an idiot though there had been no need to rub it in. He was, after all, Borelli's superior and should have been treated with some respect even if he didn't warrant it. He transferred his smile weakly to the woman staring at him from across the counter. He wondered how old she was. Her looks were so desiccated she could have been any age between eighty and a hundred. She reminded him a little of pictures he had seen in a magazine showing the remains of a mummy recently excavated from a newly discovered Egyptian tomb. He glanced down at the card lying on the counter in front of him, picked it up and scanned it as if he hadn't already seen what was printed there and dropped it again although he didn't take his eyes off it. His fingers tapped the desk top until he lifted his hand and turned it over to inspect his nails. It was better than looking at her. She appeared to be deteriorating by the minute. He half expected her to melt or turn into sand running all over the floor. So all right, the card informed him that her name was Madam Rosetta and that she was clairvoyant, could read the Tarot, tell fortunes and forecast the future but there were plenty, Borelli thought, of that kind of charlatan around. He wasn't the kind to be taken in by that sort of superstitious nonsense. Borelli was a pragmatist and wasn't even taken in by airy-fairy religious nonsense. If you can see it, feel it, taste it, hear it, touch it then it's there. Otherwise forget it. What happens when you're dead? Nothing happens when you're dead. Dead is dead, or so he firmly believed anyway. No seeing, no hearing, no smelling, no tasting, no feeling, so why do so many believe in a life everlasting? Wishful thinking, that's all, just wishful thinking.

He eventually plucked up the courage to look at her again. She wasn't that much taller than the counter and her head had fallen forward so he could no longer see her face, just an unruly tangle of grey hair and he wondered if she was actually still with him. It would solve a lot of problems if she were'nt. Or would it? Not a very good idea to have people dying in police stations, starts all sorts of ugly rumours. But then, if she weren't, he would never know what the future held. At least, in her clairvoyance what she saw the future holding even though, he assured himself, he wouldn't believe it. He gave a gentle cough, more a clearing of the throat and, as that got no reaction, it was followed by a proper cough, loud enough to echo slightly off those bare walls in that fairly bleak and empty room. He wished Antonio would hurry up with the coffee. He had been what seemed an interminable time going about it. How long does it take to heat water to make a cup of coffee? He was relieved to see her raise her head with what seemed to be a great effort and he still didn't like the way she looked.

'Well now, Madam Rosetta,' his voice was quietly encouraging, 'would you like to tell me what all this is about and why you think it is a matter of such urgency that the police should be involved?' He looked at his watch. 'Take your time,' he said, hoping she wouldn't, decided he had stood long enough, pulled up a chair and sat down.

'Murder!'

She screamed it so loudly it almost knocked him back in his seat which wouldn't have been too difficult to accomplish as he was balancing backwards on two back legs at the time. He hastily dropped the chair forward, its front legs hitting the floor with a bump and he stood. She clutched at her chest once more.

'Don't let them fool you!' She yelled.

It took him a while before he could reply. He wondered why her yell hadn't brought Antonio scurrying back to see what was going on. 'Are you telling me that someone is going to try and murder you?'

'Not me. Them! Evil is everywhere. I can see it. I can smell blood. Blood has a terrible smell! Terrible, terrible!'

'You smell blood, huh! I don't smell anything in here except damp. That's probably what you can smell as well. I don't even smell the coffee. What the hell is that man doing in there? And, apart from smelling, what exactly is it you see?' He asked, at the same time thinking why was he wasting his time with this crazy woman? The sooner a doctor really did arrive with a bag full of sedatives and Antonio with a steaming cup full of caffeine the better.

'I know you think I'm mad, Inspector, I can see it in your face. You wouldn't be the first one, but people have been beholden to me ("what an old-fashioned word" Giuseppe thought) for warning them of danger and saving them from it. You are wondering why you bother listening to this crazy person, no?'

Giuseppe nodded in agreement. She was absolutely right but he didn't think it took much in the way of clairvoyance to reach that conclusion.

'But please listen to what I have to say. Just give me a moment. It might save your life and the lives of many others.'

'All right,' he said, taking his seat once more, opening his arms wide and then placing his hands on the counter so that he could push his creaking chair back again and rock while he listened. 'I'm all ears. What can you see?'

It took a moment for her to start. Perhaps she had to gather her thoughts or was wondering how best to tell her story so that this policeman, however reluctantly, would believe her. From his seated position all he could see of her was her head.

'Ever since I was a young girl I have had the same dream, oh time and time again.' She stopped.

'Go on.'

'It is night, dark, I am lying in bed, it's a strange bed, not like a modern bed at all, very close to the floor, more like a camp bed if you know what I mean...'

Giuseppe could have done without the preamble and was wishing she would just get on with it.

'...and as I look around the bare room dimly lit by the light of a single oil lamp, a small earthenware lamp such as you find in museums, like this...' She held out her hands, palms downwards with her forefingers and thumbs together in a triangle, more or less in the shape of a lamp. 'The room is tiny and I can see my mother, it must be my mother, crying over the fevered body of my little brother. He is maybe eight or nine years old and there is another boy even younger but he is fast asleep. She is preparing some herbs in a mortar for my brother to take to lessen the fever with which he is gripped. He is in so much pain, so much pain. Then the door flies open and a burly man enters. He is dressed in long robes and is followed by a majestic looking lady all in shimmering white. On her head she wears what looks like a diadem holding a crescent moon and on her arms gold bracelets from Cyprus. She commands my mother to step away from my brother's bed. "No," my mother screams, "no!" The man pushes her away and picks up my brother, light as a feather it would seem and hardly conscious because of the fever, and takes him out of the room. My mother is prevented from following. "Why my child? Why not some other?" She sobs. "This one has been chosen," the woman answers and they leave with my brother. "May you and all your children suffer," my mother screams. "May their hearts be broken as you have broken mine." As she curses them she holds up a piece of, I don't know what it was, it looked like a small sheet of metal like copper or bronze and she falls to the floor. The door seems to close of its own accord and there is only silence and that is the end of my dream.'

'So what has all this got to do with the police, Madam? You say a child has been kidnapped and the kidnappers are going to kill it? Why? Are you telling me it's a sacrifice because of some sort of cult?'

'Yes… No… Yes… but it happened so long ago, so very long ago.' She now seemed totally exhausted, virtually in a state of collapse, leaning heavily on the counter.

'Then I'm sorry, Madam Rosetta, but there is very little there to make a case so, if you'll excuse me…' he got off his chair '…I have some parking offences to deal with.'

He hoped this levity would get rid of her. She probably knew as well as he that if a couple of cars came through the town in a day it was something for all to wonder at.

'You must believe me, Inspector, you must!' Her voice was now no more than an urgent whisper.

'Yes, well if I see some mummy running around the streets I'll let you know.' Is this what he was got out of bed for? Again he looked at his watch. 'Goodness gracious me, it's almost breakfast time. What on earth could be keeping Modafferi with that coffee? Excuse me, Madam Rosetta.' He kicked his chair to one side and headed for the inner door leading to the back of the station. He turned back for a moment. 'You will be able to find your own way out no doubt. Shouldn't be too difficult seeing as to how you're clairvoyant.' He chuckled to himself as he left her but his mirth suddenly ended when he entered the back room and smelt the gas. It was just as well he wasn't a smoker. Antonio was slumped in a chair near the stove. Giuseppe headed fast for the window and struggled to open it but for some reason it seemed to be jammed tight. He looked around the room, beginning to feel the effects of the gas, saw the full kettle on the stove and, taking it up, smashed a pane. A draft of cool air blew into the room. He turned back to the stove and turned off the gas, something no doubt he should have done first of all but in these situations logic isn't always present. He was almost choking but he now turned his attention to Antonio and was relieved to find his subordinate still alive as, with a groan, he came too somewhat. Giuseppe next went to the sink and turned on a tap to fill a glass with water which he took across to the sergeant who was sort of swaying from one side to the other in his chair. Borelli held him steady with one hand whilst with the other he put the glass against the man's lips.

'Drink,' he ordered and Antonio drank.

It took a fair while though for him to become compos mentis and even then not fully but Giuseppe wasn't going to wait for ever.

'Here, take some more,' he offered the glass again but Antonio pushed it aside. 'So tell me what happened here? No, don't tell me.' He took the glass back to the sink. 'You put the kettle on the stove, lit the gas and went to sleep and when the water boiled it boiled over and put out the flames and you nearly died. Are you one big idiot or what? The whole station could have gone up.'

'There was a boy here.'

'What?'

'A small boy. I don't know where he came from but he was here. A little boy, only about... oh... about so high.' His voice was trembling and he held his hand above the floor to indicate how tall the child was. 'He was holding out his arms, like this, as if he wanted to embrace me or for me to hug him. He wasn't Italian. I think he was Greek. Same face, same race, but different clothes if you know what I mean. Sandals and wearing a chiton, I think that's what it was called, or was it a chlamys? I can never remember which is which. He had a sort of ornament on his head, like... like a crescent moon, and gold bracelets on his little arms.'

'All the saints in heaven preserve us!' Every hair on Giuseppe's arms was standing on end.

'I don't remember anything after that.'

'The woman's not a clairvoyant! Mangia merde e morte! She's a witch!'

*C*HAPTER 2

You most probably have never heard of a place called Critone in southern Italy, not too many people have, including a great many Italians, particularly those from the north who look upon southern Italy as a foreign country full of gangsters and intent on draining the north's resources, and so you may wonder if it even exists. This is hardly surprising since it was for so many years a place of absolutely no importance whatsoever. Over the past two and a half thousand years or more, from a bustling seaport and commercial centre on an important trade route from the East, it had for various reasons slowly and inexorably decreased in size until it became no more than a sleepy little town on the Mediterranean coast. One of the reasons, apart from the poverty of the surrounding districts which in the late nineteenth and early twentieth century saw a wholesale exodus to America, Australia, and South Africa, was a mighty earthquake in 1900 on the far side of Reggio from which Critone suffered the aftershocks to such an extent that, although there wasn't all that much in the way of material damage, the psychological effect was devastating and led to even more emigration. It took quite a while for the population from being almost totally geriatric to regain some sort of balance as some of the homesick returned.

Being a seaside town there was fishing of course, once thriving with nets bulging to bursting point but, as the Mediterranean became somewhat depleted, so the fishing fleet decreased in numbers and boats were left high and dry to rot. Nobody wanted them. It simply wasn't worthwhile anymore, especially after the EU brought in quotas and other countries' ships were intent on stealing as much as they could with no thought for the quotas, for the future, and in hopes that they would never be found out.

Until recently the town's most outstanding feature was the magnificent Italian Piazza. That was its original name but it had gone from being the Italian square to Victor Emmanuelle III Square, and there was even some proposal in the nineteen thirties of renaming it the Mussolini Square but that suggestion didn't get very far as not too many in this part of the country were enamoured with the fascisti though it was wise at the time to pretend to be. If there was going to be a name change they would have voted for Garibaldi but everybody knew it as the Italian Piazza so it went back to being called that. On a couple of buildings there are faded signs, almost illegible, telling anyone interested that it was once named after Italy's King Emmanuelle III, a hero who during the first world war never left his troops except for his annual two weeks leave and, when it was tentatively put to him that he could be killed, he replied "I am but one link in a chain. If I am killed there is a younger to take my place," and indeed, as though to authenticate the name as it were, in the centre of the square there was an enormous and majestic, as befits a monarch, bronze statue of the late king standing on a white marble plinth. The marble was chipped in places and grown rather grubby over the years, not just from pigeon shit, but from trodden on chewing gum and cigarettes stubbed or allowed to go out on its once pristine whiteness. There is also unfortunately too much evidence of that modern curse – mindless graffiti! There has always been graffiti. Cavemen painted on walls but at least their painting had a purpose, success in the hunt and so forth, or so we are reliably informed, but with the advent of canned spray paints and felt tipped pens, the rash has spread it would seem uncontrollably, perpetrated in many instances by mindless vandals trying to establish their identity in a possibly non-caring world that couldn't give a shit for their existence. The strange thing is no one ever seems to see who the perpetrators are or in many cases what their graffiti is supposed to mean.

The rest of the square was also laid in marble. It was an intricate design that gave the place a look of perfect symmetry although, in fact, it wasn't that at all, being narrower at one end; the end opposite the quite majestic though somewhat crumbling city hall and municipal buildings. Police headquarters were to one side and on the other the railway station, in itself quite substantial, it's buffet a good meeting place for early morning coffee, especially in winter, everyone standing around in winter overcoats and scarves, the steam rising from their cups and issuing from their mouths every time they opened them.

As far as trains were concerned, Mussolini's trains, they were still running on time according to the schedule but it didn't really matter much to Critone because only occasionally, just occasionally, one stopped there. At times bemused tourists made the mistake of disembarking and by the time they realised that this was all there was to the place the train had departed and it would probably be twenty four hours before the next. There were buses of course but they were mainly for the use of surrounding villagers and no one of sound mind and limb rode in them without trepidation, and of hire cars there were none. A taxi was available but didn't look too roadworthy either and should the unwary traveller decide to hire it, more than likely it would cost them every last traveller's cheque in their wallet.

But things were due for a change. This was all to do with the town's mayor, one Luigi Batista who was both exceedingly ambitious and a progressive at heart and who intended to restore Critone to its former glory. Like many weedy looking men of limited stature who were forced by the nature of their physique to look up to others Luigi had very big ideas. To say that he had a long struggle to get into politics and be where he was, a force to be reckoned with (some of his opponents referred to him as a tin pot dictator or a mini Mussolini), would be stretching the truth quite considerably. Critone was not a place that any young up and coming political hopeful would want to be lumbered with, not even as a stepping stone to greater things, so he was into middle age almost when he decided to go for the jackpot and, it has to be said, he did put up quite a decent campaign in order to get elected even if people knew or suspected his promises were mostly pie in the sky. But in that he was no better or worse they supposed than any other politician and he appeared to be the lesser of two evils, his chief opponent rumoured to have too close an association with the Mafia.

Despite Batista being twice elected the place was still going to the dogs, the rate of deterioration seemingly inexorable and increasing all the time. The town coffers were empty, civil servants were constantly going on strike for wages they knew they were hardly likely to get, not yet for a while anyway, but going on strike gave them something to do like standing around rather than pushing paper around.

The only other aspirant when the second election came along was a long in the tooth discredited communist whose home was littered with dusty pamphlets published in the USSR before World War II, the walls plastered with colourful propaganda posters showing smiling buxom blonde wenches driving tractors or handsome, square jawed, suntanned muscular young men with well defined pectorals, stripped to the waist and wielding the hammer and sickle or holding up the red flag, obviously blowing in a very stiff breeze as they advanced on some unseen enemy of the state. They looked like something out of an American jerk-off magazine excusing itself under the banner of physique and health and fitness before the tsunami of pornography released on the Internet to swamp the world and such innocent prudery was, like plain brown wrappings and "anything for the weekend, sir" from the barber, were no longer wanted. Nowadays you got your weekend necessities from a slot machine or quite openly without shame over the counter from any pharmacy. Girl assistants could provide your wants these days without blushing or even turning a hair and it has been that way for some time.

He possessed a portrait of Lenin but at least, good communist though he was, he didn't go so far as to have one of the discredited smiling Uncle Joe with reputedly about thirty million deaths or more to his credit. This being Italy and the town being in the state it was you would have thought a communist would have a runaway victory but this one was considered no more than a joke. One couldn't help but feel sorry for him but then it isn't everybody who can see themselves as others see them.

So Luigi had won in what was almost a whitewash and the communist went home to reread his pamphlets, wonder what had gone wrong, consider his town, as he told his wife, to be inhabited by idiots and sigh for a perfect world that would never be, certainly not with his help or in his lifetime.

The awesome size of his majority second time around, although the turnout by disillusioned voters was somewhat on the small side, gave Luigi a delusional sense of his own importance and he was determined to make Critone great again. Who knows? One day it might be singled out for special honours from the EU; cultural city of the year perhaps, something like that. After all it did have a very long history.

Somehow, against all the odds, well in fact not so much against the odds because it was his eight year old daughter who put him onto it, Luigi discovered the Internet and the European Union and, putting two and two together had, without any difficulty, secured a large grant for the rejuvenation of his mini empire. After comfortably feathering his own nest and those of a couple of trade union officials and partly paying the wages of the civil servants to quell the waves of discontent, so averting any more strikes for a while, Luigi had to decide just where he was going to start spending the remainder of this largesse, this unexpected windfall. There was a small slum area of the town that could be razed to the ground and rebuilt thus ensuring that the inhabitants would all vote for him at future elections but those inhabitants, apart from being rehoused, would have to be paid compensation on top of all the other expenditure and many of them were so old they would more than likely have snuffed it anyway by the time the next election came around so that was out. Some of the roads with potholes like mini-craters were in desperate need of repair but as so few vehicles actually used them, and the vehicles that did weren't themselves exactly up to scratch as far as road worthiness was concerned, he didn't think that was worthwhile either. The local hospital was in a state of some dereliction, sordid would be an apt word for it, and could do with an injection of funds but surely that should be the responsibility of central government and, anyway, doctors and nurses are such dedicated folk they don't mind working in less than satisfactory conditions and people are going to go on and on and on getting sick and funds don't last forever so, in the face of such perversity, the hospital lost out.

Unfortunately for Luigi the EU was under constant fire to reassess where and how or into what bottomless black hole rather, its funding kept disappearing and one day, to his horror, he was informed that a delegation touring Italy was designated to enquire into the financial affairs of Critone and he would have to justify his use of European money, or at least invent some plausible explanation as to where it might be going. It was then that he had his brilliant idea. The town had no public toilet facilities. Every major town in the civilised world except for America, where there were only comfort stations on interstate highways, had places for people to relieve themselves and where better to build a lavatory for the use of all its good citizens but in the town square? Not one that could be seen of course, obscuring the view of the king's statue and spoiling the marble paving but one underground such as, he heard, they had in parts of London, and so excavation of the Italian Piazza was started. The king's statue, to protect it from the inevitable dust such work always produces in quantity, was wrapped in heavy plastic sheeting secured by rope; the marble paving was jack hammered at the edges, lifted, marked, and carefully stored, even the pieces that unfortunately broke in the hammering and lifting, and soon it was the turn of the JCB's to go into action. It was not too long before disaster struck; that is at least there was a definite setback as far as Luigi's great plans were concerned. A human skeleton was unearthed. Luigi managed to have it disposed of with no news of it leaking out, an amazing feat in itself in a town where Chinese whispers were rampant, so no real damage was done. With a stern warning to the driver of the JCB that any word spread around about a body being found and he would be buried along with it (such was the mayor's connections), and the trade union official in charge, for another quick bung having agreed with him, Luigi thought that would be the end of the matter. But if Luigi did believe that was the end of the matter he was gravely mistaken when a second and then a third body showed up and the JCB driver was hardly likely to be buried three times so forensics had reluctantly to be called in from Reggio and, as the body pile grew and the skeletons turned out to be from a long distant past, forensics gave way to the archaeologists and work slowed until it came to a standstill. It takes a long time to dig with a trowel and sift carefully through dirt or brush it away with a half inch brush.

Luigi was beside himself as the date of the delegation's arrival drew near. He wasn't exactly tearing his hair out. He was too fond of his carefully pomaded hair as a weekly visit to the local hairdresser could prove, but all he would have to show them were the architect's plans for the toilet and piles of dirt that seemed to grow bigger every day as the dig continued. What he didn't expect, and what made him puff himself up even more than usual as he swaggered around town or stopped for coffee and to receive the salutations of sycophantic layabouts hoping for a handout, was the enthusiastic reaction of the Italian section of the EU's delegation to the fact that Luigi's workmen albeit unwittingly had uncovered the very heart of the ancient city of Critone; and so it didn't matter one jot that work on the public toilets was suspended while the treasures of the ancient city were being uncovered, no matter how long it took. The good people of Critone would have to do what they had always done – piss elsewhere.

Victor Emmanuelle III wrapped in his plastic protection now looking distinctly grubby, his rope beginning to fray, stood all alone and forlorn in the middle of what looked like a bomb site. Luigi meanwhile was negotiating a further even larger grant and it looked like he was going to get it.

****

Antonio Modaferri awoke from a refreshing siesta and for a while lay on his back with his eyes closed giving an occasional yawn. This was the best part of waking up in the afternoon when one has slept so well. He gave a couple of stretches and wondered why he was aware of a sweet smell in the bedroom. Capricia was not in the habit of using perfume. Sometimes in the hot summer weather in close proximity he fervently wished she did. He didn't know what time it was but he was feeling somewhat peckish so, after lying quite still for a while, longer than usual, he lifted his head intending to survey the room, starting with the bed itself and was startled to see it quite lavishly adorned with roasted almonds, walnuts, apples, pomegranates and day lilies. Where on earth could these have come from? It was most peculiar to say the least. Had his wife sneaked in while he was asleep and silently laid them on the bed for him to find when he awoke? But why would she do something like that? He gently turned back the coverlet and lowered his legs to the floor in order to get up. He sat for a couple of seconds looking at his naked feet, especially the right one with the bunion from when he had that bad attack of gout that put him out of action for days. Having studied his feet he looked up and it was then that he saw him. The boy was standing by the window. He was a beautiful child, fair haired and pale of complexion with piercing blue eyes. Antonio was transfixed. The boy was smiling and this time he did not extend his arms as if inviting some kind of intimacy. Instead he extended one arm with the hand open, palm uppermost. Then he closed the hand to form a fist as though clutching at something and pulled it towards himself, Antonio felt one searing flash of pain in his chest and knew no more.

Capricia came in from gossiping next door and went straight to the kitchen to dish herself up a bowl of ice cream and on to the television set. It was some hours later that she discovered her husband crumpled up on the bedroom floor. There was nothing on the bed. She let out one long piercing scream that had half the village around in seconds.

\*\*\*\*

Professa Amalia Coniglio, or Bunny to her close friends, had been despatched from Rome to head the dig. Graduate of both Rome and Athens universities with an IQ of 165, she was a walking talking encyclopaedia of classical Greece for those who didn't know their Doric from their Ionic. Of course when it was first announced that there would be a dig in Critone most of Italy's archaeologists had to look at their maps to locate the town and so, not unsurprisingly, turned down the offer of heading what was obviously a minor dig of little if any importance in what they believed to be a little hole in the back end of nowhere. How dumb can snooty academics be when they can't see what's under their noses? Did they not bring to mind all the Greek artefacts discovered on Sicily? Had none of them visited the museum in Caltanissetta on that island simply bursting with Greek antiquities that, behind their glass cases, looked as new as the day they were manufactured; pottery, earthenware, statuary, jewellery, body ornaments, weapons and armour?

As news of fresh finds in Critone was made public it didn't take too long though for people to sit up and start taking notice; in fact to actively interfere which was why Bunny had been ordered back to Rome and was preparing to meet her superiors. Had she done something wrong? Had she been negligent? Why did she feel like a naughty schoolgirl going to meet the head mistress? She knew she had done an excellent job in overseeing the dig and most importantly making exact records and inventories of all artefacts as yet uncovered. Some still had to be identified and dated of course including those two curious heads in shape rather like large mugs or Toby jugs that had caused so much excitement, but all in good time. Rome, as they say, was not built in a day but all roads lead to it and here she was in the Eternal City.

She had to admit, as she faced the large oak door with its intricately carved panelling in front of her, that she was extremely nervous and trembling slightly. Trembling that no amount of deep breathing and telling herself to calm down could get rid of.

People who heard about Bunny, her reputation and her expertise could be excused for imagining a middle-aged to elderly rather dry academic frump in khaki shirt and pants, possibly with no make-up, possibly somewhat squat with pendulous boobs. The reality was very different. Bunny was not yet thirty. She might not have been everyone's idea of feminine beauty in the cheesy pin-up or glossy model mode but she was tall and svelte and had an air about her that was always most attractive. She was also highly intelligent, so much so that some men felt threatened by her, especially as she found it hard to tolerate self-opinionated fools though was polite enough to endeavour not to show it. Yet the atmosphere in those cases could get somewhat tense to say the least. The eyes gave away her feelings. The same applied to budding Lotharios who tried to hit on her and who were so sure of themselves they were never willing to take no for an answer.

She was not the pampered favourite of loving parents because she was a girl. Both she and her brother were consequently adored but never pampered. Her father an eminent surgeon and her mother a cellist of renown made sure she grew up the way they wanted but without obviously pushing and were delighted when at a fairly early age she started to take an interest in archaeology which was to became the love of her life. The household was sophisticated enough to allow the occasional hairpin to drop when the occasion seemed ripe and Bunny's mother was fond of sometimes coming out with a risqué story; like one that was a favourite about the world famous conductor Sir Thomas Beecham who when ticking off a lady cellist in the orchestra turned his well known and much feared glare on her and said, "Madam, you have one of God's finest gifts between your legs and all you can do is scratch it." This was sometimes greeted with gales of laughter. If the occasion had been misjudged, though this didn't happen too often, it was greeted with silence, now and again with incomprehension. Sometimes her husband would raise an eyebrow but he never chastised her and even when quite young Bunny found this particular story hilarious and giggled every time she heard it.

Eventually Bunny plucked up enough courage to knock on the door prepared to face the worst – or so she thought. This couldn't be delayed for ever.

'Enter,' a voice ordered.

She took another deep breath and opened the door.

Just as she had expected, the Dean's office was crowded. She quickly looked around. The atmosphere was not overtly hostile but it most certainly was not welcoming. It wasn't like being thrown to the lions but it was decidedly frosty. Someone, she thought, was obviously extremely miffed that she was getting all the attention and had decided to do something about it.

'Ah, good morning, Professa, please take a seat,' said the Dean with what was meant to be a smile but which was more like a snarl showing crooked rather stained teeth as he waved an antique ivory hand towards a chair. It would appear to have been specifically placed so that this looked like it was going to be more of an interrogation than the brief chat which the note she had received had led her to believe. She should have known. You did not get called back to Rome for a brief chat.

Bunny was an elegant woman who knew what style was. She was dressed in a dark blue two piece suit, silk blouse and flat but fashionable and expensive shoes but, suddenly, in front of the august gathering, though none of them showed any signs of sartorial elegance themselves, quite the opposite in fact, she felt a positive frump.

'I think you are acquainted with everybody here,' the Dean continued, extending the wave to include all the stern faced academics seated around or close to his large and formidable desk, including two of her own sex who seemed to radiate even more animosity than the men, if that was possible. There was one figure not seated, one solitary figure standing aloof as though not part of this little charade. He was smoking a pipe and gazing out of the window at something remarkably interesting in the quad below. This was the one to watch out for, Bunny thought. She didn't think the two ladies all that dangerous despite their hatchet faces but this one she felt sure would prove to be her bete noir.

'Yes,' she answered trying to control the tremolo in her voice, 'I think so.' She was about to add that she didn't know the man by the window but she didn't have the chance as the dean continued.

'Good, good. Well I asked you here today so that you can update us as to the progress of the Critone finds. I understand that some of the pieces have aroused a great deal of interest, not only in our small academic circle, but the ripples like a stone thrown into the water have spread remarkably far.' He seemed rather pleased with this simile ungrammatical though it might be. He smiled and looked around at the still stern faces of the men and women seated around him. Two or three reinforced his smile by adding their own. 'I am sure you realise, and please don't take this amiss as I am sure it is no fault of yours, that the universal media attention which one day in the future we would welcome has for now grown out of all proportion and could very well induce others to take an interest in what should be the sole prerogative of this university; interference that, needless to say…'

"Then don't say it," Bunny thought.

'…we would find most unwelcome. Yes.' He paused to take a large rather colourful handkerchief from his pocket with which to blow his nose, somewhat noisily. Bunny waited until the procedure was done with, the handkerchief replaced and the rimless spectacles that had been slightly dislodged in the process, pushed back with a forefinger onto the ridge of his rather large hooked nose.

The heads had all bobbed in agreement with the Dean's sentiments, all except for the man at the window who was still staring out into the courtyard. He was one Bunny had never seen before. She couldn't really think what the Dean was getting at and now that the nose blowing seemed to be over thought it time to put in her pennyworth.

'If I may say, Dean...' she started to reply but was cut short with a gesture of that cold hand to indicate he hadn't finished what the nose blowing had interrupted and she was not actually there to explain anything but to listen and like a good girl do as she was told.

'As I was about to say...' He stroked his beard, a gesture everyone was familiar with, it indicated a seriousness of purpose '...I have been led to believe you have already contacted somebody at the Athens Archaeological Museum regarding one or two particular items found. I would like to know what the precise reason was for this and why you yourself or one of our own resident experts could not have arrived at a conclusion as to the exact provenance of the said artefacts.' The Dean could be quite pompous at times but everybody seemed to be in concordance because there was another universal bobbing of heads. No one actually said out loud "and quite right too."

'I have reason to believe,' she was still trying to keep the tremor out of her voice and stopped to clear her throat. 'I have reason to believe that the items to which I think you are referring have some special link to an ancient lunar cult in Greece and, if this is the case, then it is further proof that the links between Greece and Italy were more than just commercial but that we might also have taken some religious aspects from the Greeks as well which would of course be only natural.'

'Or supernatural,' someone remarked with a giggle that was quickly stopped by a look from the Dean. This was serious business here and no place for levity.

'Perhaps Mithraism or the cult of the earth goddess Kybele. This could upset the whole religious apple cart...' She was just getting into her stride but he cut her off again.

'I am well aware that the apple cart as you call it could be upset which is why you will desist from making any further enquiries into the subject.'

There was a long silence. Bunny could hardly believe what she had just heard. Was the man serious? Of course he was. He wouldn't have made that outrageous statement if he weren't. She got to her feet so fast the chair almost toppled over backwards. She was ready to explode and they were all aware of it. 'But, sir, if you will forgive my saying it, this is ridiculous! I must protest in the strongest possible terms.'

'In the light of the situation and in view of all your hard work on the project we do feel some sort of reward is called for and we are pleased to announce that as from tomorrow you will be head curator with the Critone Municipal Museum. The position has been vacant for a while and we have been asked to come up with a suitable candidate. Everyone down there is most excited at the possibility of your coming. An excellent post if I may say so.' He didn't elaborate as to who everyone down there might be but the heads all nodded once more. Bunny was now speechless. "They're like Sicilian puppets," was the thought that ran trough her mind at that moment. The man at the window turned for the first time and smiled at her. She took an instant dislike to his Don Ameche style moustache.

'It is indeed a great honour to be bestowed on someone so young,' the Dean blandly continued, 'and I am sure you will prove yourself worthy of it. Thank you for your visit.' The interview, brief as it was, was apparently over, but not as far as Bunny was concerned. She hadn't expected anything like this. True in her enthusiasm she may have overstepped the mark a bit by engaging in a dialogue with Athens regarding the boys' heads but this reaction was totally insane.

'Surely we can talk...' about this was what she wanted to say only to be cut off for the last time.

'No, there is nothing more to discuss, Doctor Coniglio. The decision has been made and the announcement of your appointment has already been posted. You could of course refuse it if you so wish. That would be entirely up to you. Good day to you.'

Bunny stood for one moment and then, hopefully withering them all with as scornful a look as she could muster, she turned and stalked from the room, slamming the oak door behind her, too solid unfortunately to have much effect, and then leaning back on it. She hoped the sound might have caused a heart or two in there to miss a few beats but didn't really expect it. She wished she had worn high heels so that she could have clickity-clacked all the way out of the silent room to show how she felt but academics are made of sterner stuff usually in a little world of their own and the gesture would more than likely have gone over their heads. She heaved an enormous angry sigh of frustration. Inside the room on the other hand there was a collective sigh of relief that the interview was over and they had got away with it.

Bunny picked up her hat, coat, and the briefcase she had left on a chair outside the office and stormed out of the building, heading straight for the railway station and the express that would take her all the way back down south. Before she caught it however, there was time for a strong black coffee. It would either settle her nerves or jangle them even further than they already were. Eventually after this disturbing encounter her breathing returned to something like normal, so this was it; her career brought to a sudden and unexplained full stop, why? Farmed out as curator to a provincial museum which probably meant selling tickets and closing up shop every evening. That was of course if anyone was interested enough to enter in the first place. She held back the tears as she gulped down her coffee. What could she do? By now that weasel of an assistant she had been lumbered with was probably at this moment lording it over everyone at the dig. "Oh, yes," he would say, "The Professa has been promoted so I am in charge here now." She could just hear the slimy whining nasal little shit. Was it he who was the informer, passing on information to Rome, keeping them up to date with the findings?

She finished her coffee, put down her cup, and looked at her watch. She had previously thought she might do some sightseeing in Rome but certainly didn't feel like it now and she was about to leave for her train when one of the men she saw at the meeting entered the station. An elderly mousy looking gentleman he blanched slightly when he saw her but inclined his head in acknowledgement and then tried for a quick getaway but Bunny wasn't having it. He was scuttling towards a platform for a suburban train when she caught up with him. He stopped when he felt her hand on his sleeve.

'Er... my train...' was all he could think to say. He was actually trembling quite visibly. Bunny thought, strange thoughts pass through minds at times like this so she didn't know why she thought it, maybe it was the ancient shabbiness of his suit, the scuffed suede shoes, wrinkled shirt, egg stained tie, but she thought he had never had anything to do with women before, apart from his mother that is and perhaps a sister or two, maybe aunts, maiden and otherwise, and she had better tread warily in case he fainted on the spot in sheer terror. 'Er... my train...' he said again.

'This won't take a second,' Bunny assured him. 'I have only one question to ask you. The man who was standing at the window, the one smoking his pipe, who was he?'

He frowned. 'I don't think I recollect anyone standing by the window.' He made a point of looking at his watch and then at the platform where his train was standing.

'Very tall, about forty five, fifty I would think, salt and pepper hair, thin face, moustache, brown jacket, grey flannel trousers, red tie.'

'No... no...'

'You must have seen him!' Bunny sounded really agitated now. A couple of people passing by turned to look and this frightened the poor fellow out of his wits so that he blurted out, 'Yes, yes. I know who you mean, I think. That was Enrico Agostino. Yes, that's who it was. Yes. Excuse me, my train...'

'Agostino? The world famous archaeologist?'

'Er... yes... I suppose he is that. Yes.'

'And he will be taking over my dig I suppose. It's all decided hmn?'

'Yes. I'm afraid so. Now if you will excuse me, I really must hurry or I will miss my train.'

Bunny realised she still had a hold of his sleeve and now she let go. She must have looked forlorn because he shook his head as he left, mumbling, 'I'm sorry. I'm really sorry.'

But Bunny didn't even hear it. In fact she didn't even see him go. At last her tears had their way but it was going to be only a brief weakness. She slowly made her way to her own platform. There was a lot of thinking to do and a long train journey was just the place to do it. Any thought of sightseeing in Rome flew out the window.

\*\*\*\*

Giuseppe Borelli was having a really hard time. He had walked the town it seems for hours, questioning everyone and anyone he came across. 'Do you know a woman named Madam Rosetta? Supposedly a clairvoyant.' No, he couldn't give a surname because it wasn't on her card and no he didn't recollect it was ever mentioned. When he had returned to the interview room after rescuing Antonio from certain death he discovered she had left and taken her card with her. A description? Ah, if only the station had modern facilities, if only he could have got an artist's impression, an Identikit, a very modern computer generated image but no such luck, he had none of these things. He tried hard to give as accurate a description as he could but it all sounded rather nebulous and people just shook their heads. How many small, thin, grey-haired, middle-aged to elderly women are there in Italy? It was without doubt that proverbial needle in a haystack. His feet were sore and he was beginning to wish he was the clairvoyant. He needed desperately to talk to this elusive woman who appeared at the police station in the early hours of the morning with her bizarre story and who now seems to have disappeared off the face of the earth, well at least off the face of his home town and surrounding area. He was a very worried man.

He eased himself into a chair in Umberto's café and ordered a grappa and a coffee, then he slipped off his shoes to free his aching feet that had swollen from the heat and all that walking. Giuseppe was young and the trouble with being young and vain, he thought, is you wear shoes that are fashionable and one size too small and this is the result; but he didn't want people to think because he was a policeman that he had big flat feet and he didn't usually do quite so much walking. After all, what are squad cars for but to ride around in?

When Giuseppe entered his café, Umberto had been sitting at a table enjoying a game of cards with a group of friends with packs of cards that had definitely seen better days; dog-eared, cracked and stained as they were from much use. There were three packs in all but they were all in much the same condition, the result of spilt foodstuffs, liquids and nicotine stained fingers. An argument that had been in full spate looking and sounding as if it were about to come to blows, half the fun of playing cards with friends, suddenly stopped and there were all around nods of recognition in Giuseppe's direction. He gave a general wave in return from his seat in one of Umberto's ancient somewhat rickety chairs, if anything as rickety as those in the local police station. It was not only his feet that were sore. Giuseppe, fit though he was, was even beginning to feel an aching bum from all that walking.

He sat patiently waiting for Umberto to get up and see to him. At the moment there didn't seem any point in hurrying. As far as he was concerned he'd done all the walking and looking he was going to do for one day. Maybe he should pray to Saint Anthony. His mother always prayed to Saint Anthony whenever something went astray and, although the saint might be good at finding things like maybe a lost ear-ring, Giuseppe didn't feel he was up to conjuring Madam Rosetta out of thin air or luring her from wherever she was hiding.

Umberto finished playing his hand and stubbed out his cigarette before getting up to take and see to Giuseppe's order of grappa and a coffee. The only other person in the café was a virtually toothless ancient by the name of Alceste. Nobody knew exactly how old he was and he wasn't telling. If the truth were to be told he probably didn't know himself but the bets were on well over a hundred. A hundred and five seemed to be the favourite figure. Some people pushed the boat out and made it more than that but not by much. There is after all a limit as to how far an old body can go. Old, Alceste might be, but Methuselah he was not. He had no immediate family having outlived them all, though evidently there were some great nephews or great great nephews or grandchildren somewhere who sent him small amounts of money to bolster his meagre pension so he could have his little extras, like coffee at Umberto's and small extremely strong black cheroots that should by rights have put paid to him many a year past. His lungs simply had to resemble soot laden chimneys that hadn't been swept in years. He was looking at a newspaper. He was in the café every day to look at a newspaper but, as with his age, no one could be sure he was actually reading what he was looking at or merely pretending to as his eyes were particularly rheumy and he never wore glasses though, if he weren't reading, no one wanted to disabuse him by asking about it. If someone had called out, "Hey, Alceste! What's in the news today?" He more than likely wouldn't answer which proved nothing either way. He hadn't acknowledged Giuseppe's entrance so presumably he was so engrossed he just didn't see it or, more than likely, just didn't want to see it or what was even more likely, saw it but decided to ignore it.

Umberto advanced on Giuseppe's table and put down the grappa and coffee. He had wound up the old gramophone with the *His Master's Voice* type horn that sat on a bamboo table against the wall under a print of *The Bleeding Heart* just the customer side of the counter. The edges of the table were well burnt by smouldering cigarette butts temporarily left there and sometimes forgotten. Umberto placed the needle on the record already on the turntable. It was a bit scratchy. These old needles were now hard to come by but nobody thought to say, "Hey, Umberto, you know you can get wonderful new machines now, why do you keep that old thing?" To which his reply would have been to play his favourite old Beniamino Gigli records that he had owned for more years than he could remember and now here that famous tenor of yesteryear was singing again, faint and scratchy but still singing *La Mattinata* as he had done countless times before, blunted needle and scratchy old record notwithstanding. This was a good record. The needle never got stuck. On some of the others in Umberto's collection it needed the occasional nudge to get it out of the groove. Not too hard a nudge because that would only make the scratch worse. Sometimes it even necessitated lifting the needle right off and carefully replacing it where it could go on happily playing.

After his first mouthful of drink Giuseppe decided he had settled the dust in his throat and he could actually speak.

'I'm looking for a woman,' he said, presumably addressing everyone.

There was considerable laughter from the card table that seemed to Giuseppe to go on an inordinately long time before dying away. Was it that funny?

'So what's your problem?' One of the men, Francesco by name, said when the laughter had died down, scratching the stubble on his chin with one hand whilst surveying his cards held in the other. 'You're young, you're a good looking boy, you've got a full time job; shouldn't be too difficult for you. The world is full of women. Too many sometimes I think'. He selected and laid down a card. 'And some of them are hot for anything in a uniform.'

'You might not have noticed but I don't wear a uniform.'

With nods and grunts they had all agreed with Francesco's summing up as they inspected their own hands and the card on the table.

'Wait till you get to our age,' chipped in another, laying down his card with a deft flick of the wrist, 'then that's when the trouble starts.' He took the trick and laid the cards next to the tricks he had already won. He seemed to do everything with a flourish. 'By then, you've probably got your woman. Had her for years and wished you hadn't.'

This elicited more laughter and old Alceste giggled, revealing pink gums and the one tooth he had remaining. He might be almost blind but he certainly wasn't deaf which was just as well because, as the oldest inhabitant of the village, he would turn out to be the only one with possible knowledge of who this Madam Rosetta was.

'No, listen,' Giuseppe said, 'this is serious. A woman came into the Maroccia station a couple of nights ago yelling blue murder, that is she was saying there was going to be a murder, or murders. Yes, more than one murder. Said she was a clairvoyant and she could see it all. Of course I didn't take much notice. I just thought she was crazy know what I mean? The world is full of crazies.'

They all nodded once more and another card was about to be put down but second thoughts caused it to be withdrawn and another to take its place. The trick was still lost.

'Then she described a woman she saw in dreams and Antonio who was supposed to be making coffee at the back left the gas on and was practically asphyxiated. Fortunately I got there in time to turn it off but a fat lot of use it did him because he went home…' forgetting his beliefs for a moment, Giuseppe hurriedly crossed himself' '… and died of a heart attack. Poor fellow. But he said he'd seen a boy in the back room who he described and I am here to tell you now, the boy was dressed, I mean there was no boy of course, no of course not, but in Antonio's imagination, the boy was dressed exactly the same as the woman in Madam Rosetta's dream as she described her to me. You don't think that's crazy or what? She must have put it in his mind before he called me, before I got there. Yes, that would explain it. She put it in his mind. She was that kind of woman. So I dashed back to the interview room but she had gone. The woman's a witch or she knows something I need to know, which is more like it because I don't want to believe in witches, and I have to find her.' His speech over he took another sip of his grappa. It was hard work trying to get through to this lot still intent on their card game and probably resenting the disruption.

'Why?' This from Umberto who had left the game because Gigli wasn't singing any more and he wanted to put on another record.

'In case there is something in what she says.'

'But you said it's a load of rubbish so why not just leave it alone? You go poking around there, putting your snout in where it's not wanted, you're opening a whole other can of worms.' He started to wind up the gramophone.

'I'm a policeman,' Giuseppe objected, 'I've got to follow it up.'

'Why?' He lowered the needle onto the record. 'Was there anything in writing?'

'No, but...'

'Well there you are then.' And he went back to his game as *O Sole Mio* was heard coming from the gramophone but he obviously couldn't concentrate and was immediately on his feet again.

One of the card players decided to join in the conversation. 'If it was me I wouldn't bother. They're all crazy in Maroccia. Still living in the nineteenth century.'

'What did you say her name was?' This was from Alceste who had been listening to the conversation with great concentration.

'Madam Rosetta.'

'Rosetta... hmn... Yes...'

Giuseppe was suddenly hopeful. He waited but not for long, only until his patience ran out which was about a minute or just over and a minute can be a long long time. 'Yes? Yes? Come on. If you know something, old man, then spit it out.'

Umberto, having evidently decided he didn't want *O Sole Mio* at this moment, it didn't suit his mood, and another Canzone Napolitane, *Core'ngrato*, issued forth from the ancient machine eliciting a sigh from Umberto as he went back to his game yet again. Umberto, a widower, had been a lovesick prepubescent, a lovesick teenager, a lovesick young man, and would probably be still lovesick into his nineties should, God willing, he live that long. He glanced at himself in the mirror behind the counter as he passed and wondered what had happened to his hair that was once so lush, so black and shiny that, in its turn, it elicited sighs from all the girls.

'It was when I was very young, long before your time, or any of you other whippersnappers.' Alceste said.

Umberto stopped dead in his tracks and, instead of gazing at himself in the mirror, he turned wide-eyed towards Alceste.

There was a chorus of grunts from the card table. Men of sixty and over are not used to being referred to as whippersnappers. If it had been anyone other than old Alceste they would have been highly offended.

'Umberto,' one of the men shouted, 'give that old man a drink. It might loosen up his tongue a bit.'

'Or loosen up something else.' Bartolo, known to be the joker in the pack, the life and soul of any party, said with a grin, and they duly laughed at his quip. Alceste was not amused however at being referred to as "that old man" but he wasn't going to say no to the drink and pretended he hadn't heard.

'She was very beautiful.'

They waited.

He was the very centre of attention. He was going to milk this for all it was worth.

'Who? Who was very beautiful?' Giuseppe asked, growing a mite impatient. 'Madam Rosetta? Is that who you mean?'

Umberto, who had momentarily taken his seat, rose once more to fetch Alceste his drink, listening to the conversation as he passed.

'Yes, she was as well, a beautiful child but no, I am talking about her mother. Do any of you remember her mother? You were all no more than kids at the time. Hesper Accurso. What a beautiful woman,' Alceste made a shaky feminine outline with his hands, 'like a Greek goddess, like Aphrodite herself.'

'We'll have none of that pagan talk in here thank you,' Umberto said, frowning, crossing himself, looking at the picture of *The Bleeding Heart* and about to restart the record that had come to an end.

'I would like to have married her, that's a fact, but Achilles got there first.' He shrugged and, as a shot glass of prickly pear liqueur, his favourite tipple was placed in front of him, he lifted the glass and took a sip, rolling the liquid around his mouth and wrinkling his nose in approval and then continued. 'And why not? He was very handsome, Achilles. Everybody fancied him. There was nobody he couldn't have if he wanted. He even fancied himself.' Alceste giggled again and looked at his empty shot glass. The liqueur seemed to have disappeared very quickly and it seemed he was wondering where it had gone to. Umberto got the hint and, still holding the bottle, poured out another. He looked enquiringly at Giuseppe who shook his head so went back behind the counter.

'Besides,' Alceste continued, 'he came from a good family and had money. I had nothing. Ah well, that's all in the past, isn't it? No good having regrets. I considered myself lucky to be his friend until the day he stole my woman from me. It didn't turn out too well in the end anyway.' He went back to his newspaper. Giuseppe could hardly believe it.

'Old man...'

'Who are you calling old man?'

'I am calling you old man. You haven't told me about Madam Rosetta.'

'Have I not?' He put down the paper. 'Let me see now… a beautiful child. Yes indeed, like a rare flower, a rare rose, like her name.'

Giuseppe glanced heavenwards and all but wrung his hands. He signalled to Umberto. 'Give him another drink, this time on me.'

'That could be a mistake,' Umberto said. 'That could fog his mind completely.'

'Or loosen his bowels.' Bartolo said and got another automatic round of laughter.

'I'll take a chance on it.'

'Vabene. On your head be it.' He filled the glass and Alceste nodded his approval as he picked it up, carefully so as not to spill a drop. There was another short wait until he put the glass down again. By this time the game of cards has come to a standstill as everyone waited for Alceste to continue. A feeble example of wit can raise a smile or even a chortle, not enough to interfere with a serious game of cards, but a good story is a good story.

'Yes. There was some trouble in the village and a woman who had set her sights on Achilles and lost out to Hesper never got over it. Very spiteful she was, so she started to whisper, started to spread rumours, a sort of womanly vendetta if you like. Isn't there an old saying about a woman scorned?'

'What sort of rumours?'

'Oh, the usual stuff. You know what a small village is like. It wasn't Rosetta they were talking about but her mother. They were saying that Hesper was a witch.'

'And people believed it?'

'Why not? People will believe anything they want to believe. If people wanted to believe she could call up the devil in the form of a viper that would crawl up your arse while you were asleep and bite you so nobody would know how you died, who's to say it wasn't true?'

'True, too true,' Umberto said sadly, shaking his head. He still hadn't dropped the needle on the new record he had selected and the game was still in suspension. The conversation was too interesting.

Giuseppe didn't think vipers, being legless, could actually crawl but didn't want to interrupt the story by putting Alceste right. He also thought a viper couldn't actually do what the man suggested without waking you up with one hell of a fright before it got anywhere near where it was supposed to be going. That is of course unless the witch had cast a spell on you so that you stayed asleep or was sort of paralysed; but his mind was wandering and, thinking of snakes, he didn't like the direction in which it was going. Alceste was talking and he wasn't listening and that is how clues are overlooked.

'Matters started to get really out of hand', Alceste continued, 'everything that could go wrong in the village went wrong. It got worse and worse and it was whispered she made it happen, and stones make handy weapons. One day there was no bread in the village. The baker said he couldn't light his oven. Every time he tried the fire just went out. If you ask me he overslept because the night before he was tight as a tick and there wasn't a cat's chance in hell he was going to get up at four in the morning to start baking, but there you are, if he had no one to blame he was in big trouble and the fools believed him. At last Achilles decided if he couldn't protect his wife any longer, and there was the child to think of, by now she was being bullied at school. You know what kids are like, especially when they've been listening to what the grown-ups say. They would have to leave, and they did. They stole away one night and were never seen again. Nobody knows where they went to.'

Alceste rose somewhat unsteadily to his feet. Obviously his story had come to an end and the triple liqueur had almost done for him. There was a sort of universal sigh and a variety of facial expressions as the card players prepared to restart their game, suspended while they had been listening to all this. The old man started for the door.

'Wait a minute!' Giuseppe yelled at the departing back as bent as a sickle. 'You haven't told me about Rosetta.'

'Of course I have. Her name would be Accurso, wouldn't it? Rosetta Accurso, unless of course she got married, then her name would be different and who knows what it would be?' He gave a shrug and went on his way.

'Okay okay! But where do I find her?'

'Oh, you don't,' the voice came floating back, 'not if she doesn't want to be found. She will find you.'

*Funiculi Funicula,* a little more upbeat started to play.

****

Vincenzo Lombardi, an easy going young man, a little on the tubby side from too much enjoyment of pasta in all its many forms and a member of the dig as well as being a personal friend, was waiting at the station for Bunny's train to arrive. Although he had no idea of what had transpired in Rome, he had a suspicion all was not well and, if not sight-seeing, this was the train on which she would be returning, or so she had informed him. He was taking his chance she would be on it and he would get the news immediately and straight from the horses mouth as it were. He was not however prepared for the tornado that greeted him as Bunny stepped down from the carriage causing quite a stir in the near vicinity, departing passengers giving sidelong looks as they passed. It was not every night a banshee appeared on Reggio's railway station.

'Where is the little shit?' She almost screamed, 'I'll kill that weasly little bastard!'

'Who?' he asked, although he knew exactly who she meant.

'Don't play games, Vincenzo, I'm not in the mood. You know who!'

There was no lowering of the decibels. A few more heads were turned in their direction a little to Vince's embarrassment.

They were walking towards the exit and her pace was just that little bit too fast for him. It seemed she couldn't get her fingers around a certain throat fast enough.

'Calm down, Bunny!' He pleaded. 'Going on like this is not going to help the situation.' "Whatever the situation might be," he thought. But any attempt to placate her was going to be futile. 'Is this all to do with Salvatore?'

She stopped and turned so abruptly he almost ran into her.

'Salvatore? You bet your sweet life it's all to do with Salvatore.' Then she started off again at an even brisker pace. 'I'll Salvatore him when I get my hands on him.'

'He's gone for the weekend. Said his mother was ill and needed medical attention.'

Again she pulled up but this time he was ready for it.

'His whole bloody family will need medical attention when I'm through with them.'

'Bunny, before we go any further, tell me what happened.'

Having turned away she turned back to face him. 'What happened? I'll tell you what happened. Ever hear of a man named Enrico Agostino?'

'Of course.' He shrugged. 'Everyone's heard of him.'

'Well he's taking over the dig and it's all thanks to that sneaky little bastard sending dispatches to Rome behind my back as to what we've been coming up with.'

'You don't know that.'

'Don't I? Well when we see him let him deny it to my face if he dares. Come on let's get out of this bloody station and go have a drink.' She started off once more.

'He most probably thinks he is going to take over.'

'Who?'

'Salvatore of course. He's always wanted to be top dog.'

'Well as far as I'm concerned he is top dog, right in the doghouse and no mistake.'

'But what about you?'

'Me?' Bunny stopped and let out something that was meant to be a laugh but in fact sounded more like she had a bone in her throat and was trying to get rid of it. 'If he's the dog, I'm the donkey put out to grass.'

'What do you mean?'

'Meaning that as from now I have nothing whatsoever to do with the dig but am curator of the Critone museum.'

'I see.' Vincenzo pursed his lips while he thought about this. 'Just like that,' he said. 'Well I tell you what, for now let us just go and have that drink while we decide how best to cope with the changes and then I'll drive you home.'

'You're so bloody calm, Vince. Don't you want to kick the little shit right up his arse?'

'Yes. But what good would that do? What's more important than administering corporal punishment of any kind is what are you going to do?'

'At the moment I don't know, Vince. I just don't know.' By now under his soothing influence she seemed to have calmed down somewhat though she was keeping the tears at bay. 'What can I do? I either accept or I resign and then who is going to employ me. You can bet your last lira any post I would be up for would be forewarned. I probably wouldn't even get as far as an interview.'

'There are other places apart from Italy.'

'This was my dig, Vince, mine, and you know how important it is now that we've found those two heads. There's so much more I want to do.'

'So then you accept with grace and dignity and, in doing so, you grind salt into their wounds and dump sugar in their petrol tanks.'

'What on earth are you talking about?'

'Simple. Sabotage from inside. Isn't that what Salvatore has done?'

For the first time Bunny's laugh really was a laugh. 'Vince, you're a worse shit than that weasly little bastard, Salvatore.'

'That's why you love me so much but, compliments aside, my throat is asking where is that drink it was promised?'

'Let's go get it.'

CHAPTER 3

Richard sat next to his wife and gently, almost timidly touched her swelling belly. 'Are you okay, Honey?'

'Hmn...' She gave him a quick smile that disappeared as fast it had started. 'Just a little tired that's all.'

'Well it won't be long now. We should be pulling into the station fairly soon. I know, it's been a long trip, and tiring, but worth it don't you think? Once the baby's here...' He trailed off, looked at his watch and smiled at the elderly Italian couple sitting opposite them. They smiled back and nodded in approval. So nice to see a loving young couple soon to bring a new life into the world.

The train was slowing down. Richard stood up and brought their luggage down from the overhead rack. 'Dead on time,' he said, looking at his watch. He was beginning to wonder if the idea for this trip had been such a good one after all, especially when Charmaine was so close; but the doctors had given her the all clear to travel and the baby wasn't due for another five weeks so what could be the harm? A change is as good as a rest so they do say and Charmaine desperately needed one; working right up to the last moment in a high powered high stress broker's office. She needed a break and where better they decided than to indulge in a bit of nostalgia where it all started five years earlier? Reggio. Well not Reggio exactly. They never actually got there the first time, only went through it, but they decided that one day they would certainly return. At that time Charmaine had taken a year out of studies to tour Europe with a girl friend and fellow student, Sandra. After travelling around Greece they took the ferry from Patras to Brindisi. The ferry was of course mainly for lorry drivers and the girls' cabin though tiny was comfortable. In fact the shower section was bigger than the sleeping section but it didn't really matter for one night. The food on board was wonderful and so were the many admiring glances from the drivers. Throughout their whole trip Sandra had only one thing on her mind, finding a suitable male with whom to pass the time of day, and night. Until the ferry she hadn't had much success. They were too tall, too short, too thin, too fat, too ugly, too hairy, too shy, too pushy, too anything but what she wanted and what she wanted was an Adonis and they seemed in short supply. Nothing short of a Greek god, well a modern version thereof would do, and one who would treat her like a goddess. Oh, yes, there were men a plenty but Sandra was pernickety if nothing else and she certainly knew exactly what she wanted. On the boat she had found it, given the come on and flirted outrageously with her newly discovered young Greek god of a lorry driver who just happened to think she was the hottest thing on two legs. So at seven in the morning Charmaine, alone on the wide almost deserted ferry landing, watched as Sandra, complete with Greek phrase book, as though she needed language, was whisked away in her new friend's brand new truck; not exactly a prince on a white horse but as near as damn it in this day and age, she thought. They did have the courtesy to offer her a lift into town but she turned it down, three's a crowd, and the last she saw of Sandra was an arm giving a farewell wave out of the cab window. As she waited in the café for the municipal bus that seemed an awful long time in coming she wondered if she had done the right thing in declining the offer of a lift. It turned out that she had.

On that trip the girls had planned to travel by train from Brindisi to Reggio, cross over for a brief look at Sicily and then backpack up to Rome but Charmaine knew that, being on her own, this was now totally out of the question. Then the second knight errant appeared in the shape of a young Englishman by the name of Richard with floppy blonde hair and boyish good looks and together they whisked through Reggio, on to Rome, back to England, introductions to families, registry office and bijou flat in London with a mortgage they didn't even like to think about, especially now that baby expenses would have to be taken into consideration.

Sandra on her part evidently gave up all thoughts of continuing to Rome and bothering with her studies and went to live on a farm in Greece, surrounded by oranges, olives, and a hundred or more sheep and Charmaine received the occasional letter from her, the latest with news of her own pregnancy. It seemed the two babies, hers and Sandra's, would be virtually twins. The young Greek god had in that short period of time though grown somewhat on the tubby side but Sandra was nevertheless contented with her lot.

Now Richard and Charmaine intended to spend a few quiet days in Reggio with sight-seeing and playing the tourist, especially a day spent in Critone. It had come as a surprise when Richard showed her their travel itinerary but she couldn't have been more delighted. He had also booked them into the hotel where the girls all those years ago had planned to stay though they didn't make it. Although it didn't rate more than two stars, nostalgia won the day and so Richard and Charmaine walked into the Hotel Phoebe for a second honeymoon. When the girls originally decided on this hotel it was not only because it was affordable but they were fascinated by the name and thought they couldn't wait to see a hotel called Phoebe, but as events turned out then, thanks to that young Greek god, it was not to be.

To say the hotel had seen better days would be something of an understatement. The foyer come lounge was a large oval with a domed glass ceiling that not even winter rains could wash clean. In front of a glass cubicle on one side that served as an office there was a reception desk, its once pristine panelling much battered from years of knees, feet, and baggage, and the easy chairs around the little scratched glass-topped tables were of rattan and mock brown velvet where the colour hadn't faded or been stained. Circa 1920 they too had seen much use over the years. Once upon a time there would have been a palm court orchestra playing Strauss and other middle European melodies and Neapolitan song and maybe, in the evenings, jazz, but all that remained was a dais and the palms in their brass buckets dying for want of tender loving care. Faded grandeur was the order of the day but the hotel did exude a certain period charm. To return it to its former glory would take not only an enormous amount of money but also an enormous amount of will. The art director of a movie would be hard put to better it. There is a certain hopelessness that sometimes accompanies old age, not just in people but in buildings.

Fabrizio Bottecello, in rather dirty white jacket and not looking too clean elsewhere either, greeted them with a blast of garlic and in somewhat surly fashion from behind the desk. It would appear guests, other than those booking a room for an hour or so, were not all that welcome to him. It meant a lot more work and work was something Fabrizio as he grew older detested more and more. Visitors by the hour paid better and it only meant the sheets had to be changed more often and the rest of the room could look after itself. As long as the bed was clean, who amongst that lot was going to notice the dust beneath it? They never bothered to take in any of the rest of the room either so they never bothered to complain as ordinary guests had a habit of doing. He took a key down from a rack where assorted keys were hanging seemingly in higgledy piggledy fashion, dropped it on the desk and with podgy fingers turned the register around for Richard to fill in, at the same time holding out his other hand.

'Passports please.' At least he said please.

Richard duly handed them over. Charmaine, who sometimes had to travel for her company, still retained her own passport. Fabrizio picked them up and placed them in a drawer beneath the counter.

'Second floor. The lift is not working at this moment so you must take the stairs please.' He made no offer to help with the luggage. 'Go left and down the corridor to the right is your room.'

They left the reception desk and crossed the tiled floor, cracked in places, to reach the bottom of a wide elegant staircase, marble of course. Apart from Fabrizio there appeared to be no one in sight. The place was like a morgue.

'Why on earth did you choose this hotel?' Charmaine whispered to her husband once she thought they were out of earshot.

'Come to think of it now, I really don't know. Wasn't this where you and your friend intended staying? Somehow the name stuck in my memory and weird though this may sound, somehow it just seemed to choose itself. Well, whatever, we're here now, but if you want to move ...'

'No, it could be fun I suppose. I have to admit the place is reeking of atmosphere.'

'That's what I can smell is it?'

'You mean as well as the garlic?'

'Well that's a touch better than boiled cabbage on a rainy day in Buddlestone-on-sea wouldn't you say?'

'Where's Buddlestone-on-sea?'

'Anywhere in Britain where there are boarding houses, the type that has landladies, where you have to share the cruet, baths are confined to one evening a week and the front door is locked at eleven o'clock sharp.'

Their room overlooked the Via Garibaldi that ran the length of the town. A few years back the street had been pedestrianised so that every evening a great tumult of locals, as was the custom, strutted their way along it dressed in their finest, wanting to see and be seen. It was a vibrant scene enacted in many a Mediterranean city. Some, especially the young, every now and again fingering their equipment to make sure it was still there, went out looking for life. Some, especially those of more mature years who thought they had seen most everything, sat nursing a drink on the theatre terrace and waited for life to come to them if ever it was going to this late in their day, now and again nodding a greeting to a passing acquaintance.

Richard and Charmaine had stood at the door a long while surveying their room before both bursting out into almost hysterical laughter.

'Have you ever in your entire life seen a bed that size?' Charmaine asked in an awestruck whisper, not really expecting a positive reply.

'Yes, the great bed of Ware that held eight people in comfort, or was it more?'

'You could sleep eight in this one. I only hope there are no fleas.'

'The Italians call a double bed a matrimoniale. I wonder what they would call this one. Maybe it's a matrimatrimoniale.'

'The room is like something out of a museum.'

'Or Miss Haversham's mansion.'

'Or a film set.'

'Shades of von Stroheim.'

'Well, come on then, we can't stand here all evening fantasising. We ought to put on our best bib and tucker and go join the Italians out there before finding a restaurant by which time I know I will be absolutely starving.'

'After all that cake you ate on the train?'

'Well you do have to admit that was the most delicious cake. You have to agree, British trains do not serve cake like that more's the pity.'

'I admit it.'

'And you don't need to rob your bank account to pay for it either.'

Richard picked up the cases he had dropped at the door and they went in, closing the door behind them. He frowned as he saw Charmaine shiver.

'Darling, what's the matter? Are you not well?'

'No, it's all right. I'm all right. It's just that suddenly the room gave me the creeps. Silly isn't it?' She giggled, still a little nervously as she glanced around but she did advance further into the room, still surveying it as though she were in some unutterably strange place. 'The shutters don't close properly and some of the, what do you call them, slats? louvres? are broken. They'll let in the light all night and keep us awake.' She sat on the edge of the bed.

'After our trip nothing will keep us awake tonight, and to-morrow, well who will want to sleep? I'm sure there's a lot for us to see.' He had made his way to an inner door which presumably led to the bathroom. His doorway pause this time was even longer than the previous one before he found his voice. 'Charmaine, will you come and look at this?'

She got up and went over to join him and both stood staring in wonder at a complete Edwardian bathroom system of brass, copper, and ivory, looking, unlike the rest of the building, as though it had never been used. Richard whistled through his teeth.

'What do you think that would fetch in the Islington antiques arcade?'

She slipped an arm through his.

'More than we could afford at the moment but why don't we find out if it actually works?'

'Together?'

'Of course, together.'

\*\*\*\*

The National Museum in Critone was one of Mussolini's megalomaniac creations or at least, with his approval, designed by one or more of his architects, it was a monstrous piece of square concrete and marble; architecture dedicated to the common man, decorated with slogans in brass encouraging the aforementioned common man to perform great deeds of valour for the glory of Italy. The architects of Germany at the same time designed similar edifices no doubt built to last a thousand years. Hitler dreamed of completely rebuilding his home town in Austria. Fortunately for Linz it never happened.

Around the museum's entrance lobby were busts of all the great heroes of Italy from when it came into existence as a young nation in the nineteenth century. Up to that point the country had been a prize for various European factions to fight over and, as the foreign minister of Austria once cynically remarked, "Italy is not a nation. It is a geographical expression." Garibaldi put paid to all that from the moment he invaded Sicily with his tiny army so naturally his statue had pride of place with Victor Emmanuelle, Neva, even Mussolini himself, although this was a replacement as the original had been destroyed after the great megalomaniac's downfall.

Richard approached the desk and the myopic ancient sitting behind it, peering owlishly from behind the thick lenses of his spectacles. He obviously had great difficulty with his eyesight as three or four nicks from his morning shave bore witness, together with some bristles that had escaped.

'Two tickets please,' he said in his best Italian, having earlier swatted it up in his phrase book precisely for this moment, to which a shaky hand (perhaps that was the reason for the nicks) tore off and proffered two slightly grimy stubs from a slightly grimy book and mumbled what Richard thought sounded like "eight euro," which in fact is what it was. Having handed over the requisite amount and his tickets received he turned to see Charmaine directing her eyes towards the ceiling as if to say, "I told you so." Apart from the Victoria and Albert in South Kensington, every room an artistic treasure trove, she was not especially fond of or even interested in museums per se but this visit was for Richard's sake. He had heard the Critone Museum held a great many Greek artefacts and he wanted to see them. They had both wrinkled their noses a bit when they saw the town itself but now he smiled, took her arm, and they wandered off to see what the building had to offer on three floors of exhibition space.

The basement housed what many in Critone considered the special treasures of the area; two life size bronze statues hauled up from the seabed, of such magnificence and beauty one could almost swear they were alive. The rest of the museum held a great many artefacts relating to Greece and the Greek influence on the area, all very interesting but nothing spectacular as far as Richard was able to ascertain though he was particularly interested for some reason in a pair of heads with very pretty faces fashioned in what looked like large cups or jugs or maybe vases. He could have sworn the larger of the two, about twenty centimetres tall, had a smile on its face and eyes that seemed to be trying to tell him something and he would have liked to have found out more about these unusual objects. Then, as if in answer to his wish,

Bunny appeared at his elbow and made him jump as he suddenly saw her reflection just behind his in the casement glass.

The museum was not particularly busy at this moment. In fact, apart from Richard and Charmaine who had grown tired and was seated on a wooden bench on a lower landing nursing her legs that were starting to ache, it seemed there was only one other visitor. She placed a hand on her belly and smilingly wondered what her child was going to be. Neither she nor Richard were interested in having a scan to find out. They wanted it to be a surprise, girl or boy, boy or girl, they had no preference.

'I'm so sorry, I seem to have startled you,' Bunny said.

'I didn't hear you coming.'

'I see you are particularly interested in those two.'

Richard got the word interresante, it was close enough to the English but he had to explain to Bunny that he was afraid his Italian was pretty poor so she immediately switched to almost perfect English. If the visitor had been Greek, French, or German they would have received the same treatment.

'I said I see you are particularly interested in our two boys.'

'Boys?' He took another closer look, pulling in his chin as though to concentrate all the harder and dropping his head slightly to one side, and then turned a quizzical look in Bunny's direction. 'I thought they were girls. They're really so pretty they look like girls.'

'At that age is a child's sex so clearly delineated? And can a boy not look pretty? Put a boy in a frock and he could pass for a girl and vice versa.'

'In that case how do you know they're boys?'

'By the headdress. Oh I know you can't see all that much of it above the curls but in Greece in that period this type of head covering was worn only by boys.'

'I see. Are they portraits?'

'I suppose you could call them that. I am sure they're meant to be likenesses anyway.'

'Today it would be photographs to remember childhood by.'

'Yes, I suppose so.'

'You seem to know an awful lot about Greek culture, are you on the staff of the museum?'

'As a matter of fact, yes I am. I am the curator.'

'Oh! I'm sorry! Put my foot in it there, didn't I?'

Bunny laughed. 'Not at all. How were you to know?'

'Well I'm highly honoured that you should take time out to talk to me.'

'Really because you were so interested in our boys. I wondered if perhaps you knew anything about them.'

'I?'

'Yes.'

'But you are the expert. Surely it is you who should know.'

'I'm afraid not. Apart from dating them to somewhere around six hundred BC, and that mind you is still only a guess, we have absolutely no knowledge of what they are or what they represented or what they were for. They are extremely rare so naturally quite priceless. They are very recent acquisitions from the dig. No doubt you have seen it going on, in the square? I have been in touch with experts in Greece who inform me that in that entire country only two have ever been found so we are very privileged to have unearthed these. The others are in the museum in Athens.'

'Will you ever find out anything more about them?'

'Oh yes. I'm sure we will, in time if we keep on looking. Well, enjoy the rest of your visit.'

'Thank you. I'm sure we will.'

'We?'

'My wife. She's resting downstairs.

'Oh yes, I passed her on the way up. Very pretty if I may say so and when is the baby due?'

'Five weeks.'

'Congratulations.' And with another smile Bunny was gone. Richard took a last look at the jugs, because that is how he thought of them. He was even more certain that the larger of the two was trying to tell him something. If only he knew what it could be and, as he started to turn away, he thought he saw the jug suddenly filled with blood. He turned swiftly back but of course there was nothing; suddenly it felt like they had turned the air conditioning down to freezing.

****

The day had grown more than just uncomfortably hot. It was almost unbearable and Giuseppe as one of the pall bearers shouldering Antonio's coffin, was in his only for best occasions heavy serge suit and sweating most uncomfortably. He could feel it running down his back and soaking his shirt. He was fervently wishing he could be anywhere but where he was. In the first place he disliked funerals intensely. They made him think uncomfortably of his own mortality but he was there not just as pall bearer and because Antonio was a colleague, but in the vain hope that Madam Rosetta might show up and he could at last get around to questioning her, after the burial was all over of course, not during the ceremony, and providing she didn't make another quick exit.

The musicians making up the brass band and who ranged in age from fourteen to seventy or more, the sun glinting off their, in some cases battered, instruments, were playing the *Dead March* from *Saul* horribly out of tune and Giuseppe couldn't help wondering why their uniforms were so grubby, so old, so moth eaten and the frogging in such poor condition. Didn't they have wives and mothers? Or did their womenfolk, apart from cooking, spend all their time gossiping while they were knitting, crocheting, making lace? Anyway, looking at the members of the band, apart from a couple of those juniors, he also couldn't help thinking they were in a worse state than their uniforms and wondered who would be playing for them at their funerals which couldn't for some of them be that far off. It was amazing that some of them still had the puff to march, however slowly, and play those brass instruments at the same time.

It wasn't a bad turn out; quite healthy in fact if one could use that expression at a funeral. It would seem Antonio had no family other than his wife, Capricia, who was certainly doing her share of wailing and weeping and Giuseppe, who had been informed many times by Antonio of his wife's predilection for cheap and nasty TV, cynically wondered if it was because she was being prevented from watching her favourite show and couldn't wait to get back to the box. Also because most of the village had turned out to pay their last respects and it was her opportunity to put on a show of her own. There was nothing left in her life now that Antonio was gone. She wasn't a great church goer which is what many a widow finds comforting. The couple had not been up to date as far as modern technology is concerned: not for sentimental reasons like Umberto, but simply because they were in fact unable to cope with it, so they would not have been able to record a programme, let alone on a timer which would have been completely beyond them. In fact they only acquired a television set because everyone else had one and it, like its owners, was getting to be a bit on the decrepit side. Sometimes it seemed, like a recalcitrant child needing a good smack on the head to make it behave.

Father Benedict who, except for his time in the seminary,

had lived in the village man and boy for sixty odd years drearily intoned the funeral service. He had performed it many times before and would no doubt perform it a few times more before meeting his own end, and the young acolyte waved his incense about with gay abandon and eyed a pretty little girl in the appliquéed frock standing opposite him, making her blush and lower her head a little before lifting it up again to return his gaze. He suddenly realised the priest was glaring at him so averted his eyes, raised his chin and turned his attention with a look of innocent piety towards the heavens. He knew though, having been caught in flagrante delicto, when confessing, he would have to admit to lascivious thoughts, and at a funeral what is more. Also he had no doubt that Father Benedict would take the opportunity to talk to his mama which would more than likely lead to a box around the ears.

Giuseppe, having noticed all this couldn't help but smile until he saw the priest was now looking at him so he immediately resumed a sombre expression.

Unfortunately of Madam Rosetta there was no sign and the sun was beating down without mercy. If Giuseppe hadn't been on hallowed ground he would have cursed. As it was all he could do was sweat it out and wish it was all over. It seemed to be going on forever.

*****

Richard, who considered himself something of an expert when it came to museums, was quite impressed by what he had seen. In so many provincial museums the lack of information and interest in subjects could make for a rather boring visit, something most school children care to forget but, to his surprise, Richard, looking at the brochure and display cards in four languages, thought them remarkably informative and precise, giving just the right amount of information, provenance, and analyses where needed. Leaving Charmaine seated on her wooden bench, he wandered from room to room but soon he was no longer taking in what he was looking at. Always in his mind's eye was that boy's face and the overpowering image of the blood. He was almost tempted to go back and take another look at it but decided his imagination was somewhat overwrought so, instead, he stopped to inspect the walls of a room that were covered with large photographs of the local dig in progress including pictures of some of the finds, two of which were of course the Toby jugs. Once again it seemed that the boy in the larger of the two jugs was somehow pleading with him. In the photograph his look was one of terrible pain, as if the child had suffered great hardship in his few tender years, but surely it must be his imagination playing tricks again? How could the photograph show a completely different expression to the original he had seen upstairs? Maybe it was a trick of the light when the photograph was taken rather than a trick of the imagination. He noticed for the first time the small crescent shaped pendent hanging just below the neck, the few locks of curly hair escaping from either side of the hood, hair that must have been so soft and as he stood, almost as though mesmerised, a feeling of hate, despair, death, almost overwhelmed him. He turned and fled from the room.

Richard's legs were trembling so much he wondered if they would hold him up let alone move. He made it to the bench on which Charmaine was sitting and, seeing the state he was in, she was about to get to her feet when he collapsed beside her. His breath was coming in gasps as his chest tightened.

'Richard, what's wrong? What's the matter?'

'It's nothing… nothing… I'll be all right in a minute.'

'You look ghastly.'

For a while his breathing was so laboured he couldn't say anything else. Eventually it started to calm down although he still felt rather shaky. Maybe fresh air was what he needed.

'Must've been something I ate last night... given me a touch of wind.' He turned to smile at her, a smile that was meant to be reassuring but he was so pale it only increased her anxiety. She had sometimes wondered about Richard's health. There was nothing she could be certain of but, watching him bare chested while shaving for example she had been made only too aware that his breathing was somewhat laboured at times and it worried her although she never said anything. If he felt there was a need to see someone about it surely he would do so without the necessity of her telling him. He would just think she was nagging.

'I'll sit for a moment and then we'll leave,' he said. 'Just give me a minute.'

The pain in his chest seemed to be subsiding, leaving him as quickly as it had appeared, and his breathing was now that much easier. He shook his head, pursed his lips and blew out hard, wondering what could possibly have brought it on. He had never suffered any form of heart trouble. Oh, he knew there could be hidden faults that gave no indication of their presence until, without any warning; out of the blue there is a fatal seizure. So, in a way, what had just occurred was, to say the least, a little frightening but a recent physical check-up for insurance purposes had shown no sign of anything wrong so, as he said, maybe it was just a touch of indigestion.

'There's a cafeteria downstairs. We'll take a slow walk down and get you a glass of water and both of us a strong coffee maybe, and if you don't start to feel any better we'll ask someone in authority to call a doctor.'

'Well, what about you?' Richard asked, pointedly directing his gaze at her stomach. 'How are you feeling?'

'Apart from the fright you've just given me, I'm fine. I don't know about him in there though.' She gave her belly a little rub. 'You could have given him a real scare too.'

'Him?'

'Well, I can't think of it as "it" anymore, not now that he, she, is so close.'

Richard had got to his feet, steady at last, took her hand and they made their way by degrees down to the cafeteria.

****

It was all over. Antonio had been laid to his final rest with as much ceremony as the village could afford. Giuseppe had tossed his handful of earth on the coffin and hoped his compatriot was sleeping peacefully. He had certainly looked peaceful while the coffin was still open. In fact he had looked twenty or so years younger. There had been no need for an autopsy. It had obviously been a massive heart attack, or so the doctor had maintained, and he had been quite prepared without question to sign the death certificate.

Giuseppe looked around at the mourners and decided there was no one there who could give him any information but Father Benedict might just know the identity of the mysterious elusive Madam Rosetta. The last rites being over, the priest and his acolyte weren't hanging about but were already well on their way and it took a bit of a run for Giuseppe to catch up with them.

'Father!' he shouted. The boy tugged at the priest's alb and the pair stopped. Panting slightly, mainly because of the heat, Giuseppe got back his breath by blowing out hard a couple of times, hands pressing on his knees, and then straightened up and said, 'Sorry to bother you, Father, at a time like this but I wondered if you could give me some information.'

Father Benedict said nothing, merely bowed his ancient head to indicate he would if he could. Giuseppe noticed the young acolyte, who he didn't think he had ever seen before, wasn't looking at them but was facing away as his gaze followed the young girl leaving the cemetery. Giuseppe couldn't help but smile and hope the path of young love would run smooth which actually is seldom the case.

'Father, I am trying to find a lady who calls herself Madam Rosetta. Perhaps you know of her.'

The acolyte turned around and with a shock Giuseppe noticed he had blue eyes. It hit him forcibly because he could not remember anyone locally having eyes anything but brown. It wasn't that blue eyes were all that rare in Italy. There were blue eyes in the north and even in Sicily, the result of the Normans' colonising, but he had never seen blue eyes in this locale.

The boy had turned away again but by now the little girl had disappeared.

'What's your name, son?' Giuseppe asked.

The boy turned back and this second shock was even greater than the first because his eyes were brown. They were definitely brown. But Giuseppe would have sworn on his mother's life that previously they were blue. What kind of trick of the light was this, if trick of the light is what it was?

'Isadoro,' the boy said.

'Isadoro? That's not an Italian name.'

'It's Greek,' Father Benedict said. 'It is actually a girl's name, Isadora. His parents set their hearts on having a girl child, they already had three boys and they chose the name before he was born so, when their baby girl turned out to be this handsome youth, and he is handsome isn't he?' The priest gave the boy an affectionate pat on the cheek. 'They decided to keep the name, changing it to the masculine. I didn't like it of course. We owe the ancient Greeks a great deal, of that I'm sure, but as pagans they weren't exactly the most moral people in the world, not according to our Christian lights anyway; but there you are, parents get some strange fancies and you can't talk them out of it. The name actually means "gift of the moon".

Isadoro, on hearing the priest's remark about him being handsome, had turned away again but before Giuseppe could say anything else, the priest shook his head.

'I'm sorry, my son, as to your question I'm afraid I can't help you. I know of no one by the name you mentioned.'

'Thank you. Excuse me for bothering you.'

Giuseppe watched as the old man and the young boy who was a gift of the moon moved on.

****

'Two coffees please, black and very sweet.'

'Sweet?'

'Plenty of sugar.'

'Ah, sugar on tables.'

The girl, chewing her bubble gum, was giving Richard a strange look.

'He's had a shock.' Charmaine said, noticing it and wondering why she was bothering to excuse him. She wasn't sure whether the girl understood her or not as she turned away to make the coffees and Charmaine, who had taken charge and was standing by the counter, smiled encouragingly across at Richard already seated at a table and seemingly staring into space so that he didn't acknowledge her look. Then, having paid for the coffees, just in time preventing the girl from adding milk, and collecting two glasses of water at the same time she picked up the Formica tray and went to join her husband.

'How are you feeling now?' She said as she set the tray down on the table and settled herself into a chair.

Richard nodded. He didn't want to say anything in case he tempted fate.

'We'll go back to the hotel as soon as we've downed these.' She lifted her coffee cup. 'We've had quite enough adventure for one day.'

'You might as well sit for a while longer. The heavens have opened. You'll be soaked in minutes.' The advice came from Bunny who happened to be passing through the cafeteria and who paused at their table.

'Hello, again,' Richard greeted her, rising to his feet in true old-fashioned English style. He thought of saying "we mustn't keep meeting like this, people will talk," but he didn't know if she would understand he was only jesting so said nothing more. Charmaine was looking somewhat bemused.

'I'm afraid I don't know your name,' Richard continued.

'Amalia Coniglio,' Bunny told him.

'My name is Richard, Cummings, Richard Cummings, and this is my wife, Charmaine.'

'How do you do?'

'Miss… no it wouldn't be miss would it? Of course not but I don't know your title either.'

'Doctor.'

'Well, Doctor Con… Con…'

'Bunny.'

'What?'

'My friends call me Bunny.'

'I see. All right then, Bunny it is. Won't you please join us for a moment? That is if you're not frightfully busy.'

'Molto gentile,' she said, sat down and Richard followed suit but then immediately got up again.

'Oh! Can I get you something from the counter?'

Bunny shook her head. 'No thank you. If I drink another coffee today I will o.d. on caffeine.'

'Something else maybe.'

'No, thank you.'

Richard sat down again.

'So I take it you are on holiday?' She directed this at Charmaine before transferring her gaze to Richard.

Richard, about to take a sip of his coffee, paused and smiled across at his wife. 'That's right. Last time as a twosome I would think.'

Richard pointed to the obvious bulge and Charmaine smiled in turn.

Bunny returned the smile. 'Of course. It won't be so easy in future to travel with a baby.'

'Five weeks before that happens', Charmaine said.

'So your husband informed me.'

Charmaine had been wondering how these two had met and decided now was as good a time as any to ask, so she did.

'Oh,' Richard said, 'Bunny is the curator here and she very kindly stopped to inform me about certain things concerning the dig that's going on. You know, we passed it in the square?'

'Oh, yes. I see.'

'Do you know what sex it will be?' Bunny was looking at Charmaine's bump.

'No,' Richard said. 'We didn't want to know.'

'Well, I wish you joy of him, or her, as the case might be. In Greece they say when a baby is baptised, "na sas zize," may he, or she, as the case might be, live for you.'

'That's a lovely thing to say. I think it's going to be a boy.' It was Charmaine who said this with a smile. Richard looked at her in some surprise.

'What made you say that?'

Charmaine shrugged. 'I don't know; it just suddenly came into my head. I feel certain it's going to be a boy.'

Richard turned back to Bunny. 'Talking of boys, those jug things, or vases, or whatever they are; I'm intrigued, do you really know nothing about them?'

'Nothing, except I believe they may have had something to do with a religious cult we don't yet know about. A lot of research is needed there. Sooner or later I am sure the mystery will be solved.'

'They gave me the creeps.'

'What?'

'The creeps. They gave me the creeps. Do you not know that expression? They made me feel very uneasy. There is something, oh I don't know how to describe it without sounding very melodramatic, but there is something I do believe inherently evil in them.'

'Oh, Richard!' Charmaine laughed with embarrassment and looked almost apologetically at Bunny. 'Take no notice,' she said, 'he's had a bad turn.'

'They're inanimate objects!' Bunny said, trying not to smile.

'Indeed they are,' was the rejoinder, 'but with a history and the question is, what history?'

'Hmn... Strange you should feel that way. I had a lady in here who felt exactly the same way about them as you did, if not even more so. For me, they are still, wonderful finds that they are, just inanimate objects and I won't be happy until I find out exactly what their purpose was. Conjecture is one thing, definite proof another. It's a pity the season is so very short. I would like many more visitors to see them. Well, I must be getting along. I thought this job was going to be a doddle. Isn't that the right expression?' Bunny smiled. 'But in fact I seem to be at it all day long.' She got to her feet and Richard rose to his. 'Enjoy the rest of your stay in Italy,' she said, extending a hand which he took. She smiled down at Charmaine. 'Let me know how it goes when he arrives.'

After she had left, pausing at the counter to have a word with the girl there, Richard sat down again to finish his coffee by now grown rather cold.

'That's what triggered it off, isn't it?' Charmaine queried.

'What?'

'Your not feeling well. That's what triggered it off.'

'What?' He laughed albeit a little uncomfortably.

'That feeling you got, whatever it was that made you feel uneasy.'

Richard shrugged. 'I don't think so. No, not possible. Well maybe. I must admit it was all most peculiar. And I think the rain may have stopped. If you've finished your coffee shall we go?'

****

Giuseppe was seated in the local trattoria and gazing mournfully at the spaghetti carbonara gradually congealing on his plate and, in consequence, looking most unappetising. He really for once had no appetite which, for someone who enjoyed his food so much was rare and, for a moment, he played absentmindedly with the spaghetti before putting the fork down again.

His cousin, Arturo, owner of the establishment, passed by his table and stopped.

'What's the matter, Pepe? All of a sudden our food not good enough for you?'

Giuseppe looked up, shrugged, and shook his head. 'No,' he said, 'It's just I don't seem to have any appetite at the moment.'

'How come?'

Arturo sat down at the table and gave the plastic table covering a cursory wipe with his towel waiting to hear the whys and wherefores of his cousin's doleful countenance but there was only a silence.

'Well, come one, Giuseppe, what's the problem?'

'Have you ever heard of a clairvoyant woman by the name of Rosetta?'

Arturo shook his head. 'Can't say that I have. Why?'

'Well she is the problem; she is what is worrying me.'

'How come?'

And Giuseppe gave his cousin a run-down of events so far to which Arturo shook his head, picked up the plate of cold spaghetti and, with another cursory wipe of the table, headed for the kitchen.

****

The woman in question at this moment gasped and placed a hand on her chest. She could feel the uncertain rhythm of her heartbeat through her clothes. It was racing.

'Oh, God! It's happening again.'

She had been about to light the gas to make coffee but dropped the kettle in which she was going to boil the water. It fell with a loud clatter, losing its lid and sending its contents streaming across the floor, and the noise brought her daughter running into the cramped space that passed for a kitchen. She found her mother, white of face and breathing heavily, seated trembling at the table.

'What is it? Mama? What's wrong? It's your heart? I'll send for the doctor.'

For the moment, unable to speak, Madam Rosetta shook her head and waved a hand to indicate a negative then, finding her voice, 'No doctor,' she gasped, 'there's no point. It's happening again.' And then, as she tried to calm herself, 'we've got to do something.'

'What? What can we do?'

'Get the car. We'll go and see the curator.'

'Now?' She glanced at the wall clock. It was late. 'But you've already done that. She wouldn't listen to you, remember? She almost had you thrown out.'

'Please, Anna! Do as I ask. Just get the car, will you?'

For a moment Anna stood irresolute, regarding the older woman almost in despair. She knew her mother had the gift but sometimes it was so much more of a burden than a blessing. She hadn't been told exactly what her mother was experiencing but she realised, whatever it was, it was dangerous and she feared for her mother's life. One day, possibly soon, the heart must surely give out.

'Well, let's hope this time she listens to you.'

'She must, she must. Before it goes any further she must listen.'

*C*HAPTER 4

Richard sat on the bed looking down at himself and slowly unbuttoning his shirt. It would seem the air conditioning had irrevocably broken down. He was wondering what the hotel did as far as laundry was concerned, if anything, and having slipped off the shirt, he took a rueful look at the armpits but resisted the temptation to sniff. Maybe they would find a laundrette; otherwise they would run out of clothes fast and the chemist would run out of deodorants. Socks weren't a problem. He wore sandals and had already slipped them off, besides which things like socks, even underwear at a push, can always be rinsed out in the bathroom. Back in London Charmaine seemed to be forever doing it. He smiled as a vision of stockings hanging over the bath to dry flashed through his mind.

'Did you see those two women on the stairs?' He shouted to an unseen companion. 'I'm sure they're on the game.'

'They most certainly are,' Charmaine answered, sticking her head around the bathroom door, 'only they aren't women.'

'What?' he frowned. 'I don't believe you.' Then laughed. 'What makes you think that?' He was laughing too because he always thought she looked rather ridiculous in a plastic shower cap, cute but ridiculous.

'Have you ever seen a woman with five o'clock shadow?' The head disappeared.

'No!' he shouted back, 'But I've seen them with moustaches!' He threw the shirt on the floor. The head, still in its plastic shower cap, reappeared.

'With an Adam's apple the size of a walnut?'

'I wasn't looking that high.'

'Men! You're all the same. The slightest glimpse of a thigh and you've got the hots. Well, my dear, with those two you would have got a lot more than you bargained for.' She almost sang the last five syllables so he decided to join in with a tune of his own, 'Not looking so high, I catch a glimpse of thigh, and then suddenly I've got the hots.' He performed a little dance to accompany himself by tapping his bare feet on the carpet. 'How'd you like that? What did Cole Porter have that I haven't?'

'Talent and a musical ear. It won't make Eurovision that's for sure or, if it did, it would be nul point. It won't make any talent show either. Let's face it, darling you wouldn't make a tunesmith in a hundred years. Don't let the Italians hear you singing. You're likely to be deported. Anyway, I'm glad you're in such high spirits again. I really was so worried. I take it your yodelling means you're feeling a bit better?'

'Much better thank you. Can't think what it could have been. Gave me quite a turn I can tell you.' He looked down at himself again. There wasn't an ounce of fat on him. In fact he was in peak condition. He would have liked to have had more colour instead of the milky whiteness that was his skin, the result of the English weather, but maybe over the next few days he could soak up some sun, keeping in mind that overdoing it and getting burnt as so many did could completely ruin their holiday.

'It gave your little wife quite a turn as well.'

There was a sudden burst of laughter from the corridor.

'There does seem to be an awful lot of activity in the hotel at the moment, not like earlier when it was the Marie Celeste.'

The head appeared once more. 'What did you say?'

'There seems to be a lot of coming and going at the moment.'

'My dear, sweet, naïve innocent husband. Of course there is. It's that kind of a hotel isn't it? We probably won't get a wink of sleep all night.'

'I never knew that.'

'It's obvious you didn't.'

'Why's that?'

It was her turn to sing. 'Boys and girls come out to play; the moon is shining bright as day.'

'Stop it!'

A startled Charmaine stared at her husband. She had never heard him yell like that before. Having stood up he had now flopped down on the bed again. His face was distorted and he appeared to be trembling violently.

'Richard?' Her own nerves were jangled by his reaction. She tried to make a joke of it. 'I don't think my singing was that bad... was it?'

He seemed to calm down a little though he was still breathing hard.

'I'm sorry... sorry... darling. I don't know what came over me. I just suddenly felt...'

'I was seriously worried about you in the museum, Richard. You looked like death warmed up.'

'Thank you very much.'

'And I am seriously worried about you now. Suddenly you don't look much better.'

He had got off the bed and trotted across the room to join Charmaine in the shower. She turned back as she saw him coming.

'No I mean it,' she said. 'I almost got to asking that nice lady in the museum if she could call a doctor for us.' She was surveying the various dials and handles wondering which one should be opened first. Richard had done it all the first time.

'It was nothing. My imagination got the better of me, that's all. Come to bed.'

'A one track mind. I'll take my shower first and, if it's all right by you, I'll have the side nearest the windows, there might be a bit of a breeze. You would have thought all that rain would have cooled the place down a bit or they would have repaired the air conditioning. What did the man downstairs say?'

'To put it as succinctly as possible, no can do.'

'"No" would have been more succinct. On second thoughts you have that side. The light coming through the blinds will only keep me awake and you sleep like a log no matter what. No, thinking again, I will have the side nearest the window. There'll probably be a lot of coming and going to keep me awake.'

Richard laughed. 'Have you finally made up your mind?'

'Yes.'

'Well, whichever side you take it will be for one night only. We'll leave first thing in the morning', he said, 'first thing. I've decided I don't want us to spend another night in this crummy hole.'

Charmaine turned on the shower.

****

The plate of congealed spaghetti having been taken away Giuseppe was at least enjoying his favourite desert, tiramisu. That he simply couldn't resist. It had for a moment taken his mind off his worries but they came back with a vengeance. He couldn't understand it. He kept on seeing the boy's face, the boy with the eyes that were blue one moment and brown the next. Absurd, an impossibility, he must have imagined it. Perhaps he ought to see the boy again. But why? What possible excuse could he have? And what was it to him if some crazy old woman claiming to be a clairvoyant had appeared in the Maroccia police station, babbling inanities and then poor Antonio, who nearly snuffed it with the gas, is only a short time afterwards found dead on his bedroom floor evidently from a heart attack? "For God's sake," Giuseppe said to himself, "heart attacks happen, they happen every day of the week. What was so special about Antonio? For starters he wasn't exactly a youngster anymore and there had evidently been no need for a post mortem to certify cause of death. But since that brief appearance in the police station Madam Rosetta seemed to have disappeared off the face of the earth. Where could she have got to?"

****

'Hello, hello,' came the voice from the intercom, very loudly as though the owner of the voice wasn't used to these new fangled gadgets and didn't know how to treat them. Would the first hello have been enough? Could she be heard from some distance? 'Professa, it's Madam Rosetta, please please please I must talk to you!'

Despite the urgency in the voice Bunny was still determined not to have anything to do with this crazy woman. How had she found her address? It was more than annoying, it was downright worrying. She hadn't rung off but the silence dragged on until Madam Rosetta spoke again. 'Are you still there, Professa?'

'Yes, I am here though God knows why. I really do not want to see you. I told you when you came to the museum we have nothing to say to each other...'

'Oh, but we have! We have! Please! You must listen to me!'

'Madam Rosetta, I am going to ask you for the last time, please go away and do not bother me again. I do not want to hear anything more from you.'

'I will not go away. I will not. Not until I have spoken to you, said what I have to say.'

'Do you want me to call the police? Because if you don't stop pestering me that is exactly what I shall do. Now please, Madam Rosetta, go away and good night.' She switched off but there was only a moment, she hardly had time to turn away before the buzzer went again. Madam Rosetta was certainly being persistent despite the threat of the police being called. Obviously she was not going to be got rid of that easily. Bunny could either ignore the call or finally give in and let this weird woman have her say, not that she hadn't already heard it once and doubted there would be anything new to add. Now very angry, she switched on the intercom.

'Now look...'

'Professa, this is Anna speaking, Madam Rosetta's daughter. Please see my mother. I assure you she has something of great importance to say to you.'

There was a moment while Bunny's anger abated slightly and she thought about this and then, 'All right,' she said, 'I'll give her five minutes but no more.' She pressed the bell to release the street door catch and then opened the front door of her apartment and waited on the landing, leaning against the jamb, arms folded, expression grim, while Madam Rosetta slowly climbed the stairs to where she stood. It took an interminable time and Bunny was beginning to wish she hadn't agreed to let her in but eventually breathing heavily the old lady arrived. Without a word, Bunny unfolded her arms and turned back into the apartment, stood to one side, Madam Rosetta followed and Bunny, after casting a look down the stairs to see if anyone else was there, closed the door. 'This way,' she said, leading her unwanted guest into her living room. 'Where is your daughter?'

'She will wait for me by the car.'

'You drive?' Maybe this woman wasn't quite as unworldly as she appeared.

'Anna drives.'

'Yes.'

'Professa…'

'I don't know', Bunny cut her off, 'why you are being so insistent and why I was silly enough to let you in. I'm sure I will regret it but, now that you are here, have your say and make it quick. I told you at the museum that what you are asking for is ridiculous, out of the question, absolutely impossible.' Bunny was determined to make the point once and for all. 'On the other hand it could be done I suppose but, believe me, without my knowledge or it would be over my dead body.'

'Professa, that's exactly what I'm worried about.'

'Are you threatening me? I don't take kindly to threats. You can bet after what you've told me I'll have everything well and truly guarded.'

'No, I would never threaten anybody but I am warning you, though I don't think the body will be yours. But somebody… somebody…'

Without being invited to and for only five minutes some of it already gone, it seemed an odd thing for her to do but Madam Rosetta sank into the nearest chair, shaking her head as she did so. The breathing had calmed down a little but Bunny could still hear the wheezing and wasn't too sure at this point what she should do.

'Would you like a glass of water?'

Madam Rosetta waved a hand in refusal, at the same time still shaking her head.

'Something stronger perhaps?'

It suddenly occurred to Bunny that this might be the old girl's problem in which case a couple of nips and it wouldn't be too long before she was out of there and Anna could drive her home: but there were the same gestures of refusal as before then, suddenly, Madam Rosetta clutched at her chest and the wheezing now became a frantic gasping for breath. Bunny, for a moment, wondered if the woman was a consummate actor but then realised she really was in some considerable pain as she struggled to rise from the chair and she was truly worried for her. She took a chair opposite, leaned forward, frowning with concern but apparently helpless as to what to do.

'Madam Rosetta, please calm yourself. I will listen to what you have to say. I will listen. I don't say I will act on it, in fact I am quite sure I won't, but for now I will listen and think about it, then I must ask you to please go and not to worry me again.'

With Bunny's soothing tone, the breathing became easier and, after a moment, Madam Rosetta continued.

'I asked Anna to wait for me outside because I do not want her to be involved in this. She is an innocent young girl who, thank God, has not inherited this awful gift I am cursed with. Yes, Professa, I use that word advisedly, it is a curse. Right at this moment, please believe me, I would rather be anywhere but here talking to you but I have to do this. Anna does not believe it is a curse. She thinks of it as a gift, that I was chosen to do good work.' There was another pause as Madam Rosetta thought about this, then she continued, 'I know you don't believe me. You think it's all nonsense, I am aware of that, you would not be the first or the only one, but I have come to ask you, beg you, to reconsider, what we talked about the other day.'

'What you talked about the other day and, tedious as it may be, I have to repeat, what you ask for is impossible, whether I believe what you say or not. I'm sorry. Now, if you don't mind...' Bunny got to her feet, an indication the interview was over and it really had been a waste of time.

****

The remains of Giuseppe's plate of uneaten spaghetti, long removed, had been dumped outside for the alley cats to squabble over, which they were doing with much growling and the occasional swift flashing of claws, and he had indulged in a second helping of tiramisu; but he was still seated in Arturo's trattoria, having also had more vino that was good for him and not really feeling like going home.

The trattoria was now packed and Arturo, rushed off his feet, finally had to ask Giuseppe to move as he needed the table; people were waiting and they wouldn't wait for ever and that was money lost. There were other restaurants in town. He couldn't even go and sit in the kitchen. He would just be in the way. Giuseppe nodded, said his good nights, waving to Arturo's wife, Maria, who was far too busy to see his gesture, and staggered out into the night.

Without looking, he was about to step into the road when a little Fiat trundled along and he had to hurriedly step back, almost losing his balance on unsteady legs. He could make out there were two women in the car and he could have sworn one was Madam Rosetta. It would be ridiculous to say he was immediately sober. No way was he going to get rid of the alcohol in his system that fast not even with sudden shock and he stood for a long while leaning against the wall.

'Shit!' He said. 'Shit shit shit shit!' What was it Alceste had said? Something about not finding her? She would come to him? Something like that. He couldn't remember exactly.

A couple leaving the restaurant avoided him and hurried on. Swearing drunks can be dangerous. He patted his pockets but he didn't have his phone so he turned and staggered back into the trattoria. He would have to use Arturo's phone even though he thought it too late and it was going to be nothing more than a gesture. He decided it was fate, he was never destined to meet up with this elusive woman, but he wasn't one to give up too easily.

****

Bunny hoped she hadn't been too brusque in her refusal to even contemplate Madam Rosetta's strange request and was now mentally kicking herself at not thinking to question the old woman further about her so-called visions. Maybe Madam Rosetta could have given her some kind of a clue, no matter how nebulous or far-fetched it might have seemed, as to what those items meant to her but now it was too late, unless she was to receive a third visit from the clairvoyant. She was in a very unhappy frame of mind as she made ready for bed, knowing it would be a long time before she would manage to fall asleep. She tried to read for a while but found it impossible to concentrate. She kept going over and over the evening's meeting with this strange woman. She put down the book and reached out to switch off the bedside lamp.

****

The rain had stopped and what clouds remained, whipped by the wind, seemed to be scudding across the sky almost at a gallop, though on the ground no wind could actually be heard. The town gave every appearance of being deserted and the silence was ominous.

For a while the moon was still hidden but then, as one fairly heavy cloud was dispersed, a thin sliver of moonlight piercing the broken slats of the blind fell across the floor of the room in the Hotel Phoebe and moved slowly towards the bed where it fell across the figure of Charmaine lying peacefully asleep. Eventually it crept over the pillow and reached her face.

Charmaine woke with a start as she felt her unborn son kick quite violently as if suddenly awakened from a deep sleep. 'Oh, my God! It's happening. It's happening! It's too soon!' She turned to face her husband still gently snoring. 'Richard!' She shook his shoulder. 'Richard! Wake up! Contractions! They've started! Richard!'

He sat up, suddenly wide awake. 'What? What?'

'The baby! It's coming! Oh, God, why now? Why now? It's too soon!' She let out a moan that turned almost into a scream as she felt the stab of pain across her abdomen.

Richard had jumped out of bed and moved around to her side. He sat next to her, one arm comforting around her shoulders. 'Okay, okay… breathe deeply', he said knowing he was being totally inadequate. 'That's it, breathe deeply.' Furiously he was trying to remember everything he had been told at prenatal classes but without success. He leapt off the bed. 'Shit! Where are my trousers?'

'My waters have broken!' She screamed. 'Richard! Help me!'

'Stay calm! Stay calm!' He was as hysterical as she. 'I'll get help.' In the moonlight he finally located his trousers on a chair across the room from where he was standing. In his haste he couldn't at first find the correct legs, his feet kept snagging, but eventually he managed to pull them on. He could hear Charmaine's moans as he frantically zipped up. He could feel his heart thudding in his chest and, as the sliver of moonlight illuminating the room fell across him he felt the sudden tightness in his body. His hand flew to his chest. He swung around to look at his wife but it was already too late. His eyes had glazed over and his body fell to the floor.

For a moment the world seemed to stand still and then came the scream and the scream and the scream as though in the silence of the night it would echo the length of the via Garibaldi. She heard the screams from somewhere far far away it seemed but it was a while before she realised it was she who was screaming. Now she was sobbing.

'Richard… Richard… help me…' She half rolled, half fell from the bed and stretched out her hand to reach for him where he lay, his face still contorted with the pain he had gone though. 'Oh, my God! The baby! The baby! It's coming. No, please no!' She screamed once more as the baby's head appeared. The child was dead.

C HAPTER 5
The rain had started again and was now lashing down almost in sheets across the windscreen. The wipers could hardly cope with the torrent of water. Anna had been meaning to have new ones fitted and was now regretting she hadn't got around to it. She felt these were going to seize up at any moment. She leant right forward, crouching over the wheel, eyes screwed tight, concentrating as hard as she could to see the road ahead. They were out of the town now and there were no street lights to guide her. In the darkness the rows of olive trees almost camouflaged the edge of the road and a couple of times she was in danger of veering off but managed to straighten up just in time.

'So she still wouldn't listen to you?' Anna asked yet again.

'She will never listen. I will have to find another way, take things into my own hands maybe.'

'Is that wise?'

In the darkness Rosetta shrugged. Throughout life choices have to be made and she knew this thing would torment her forever if she didn't make the right choice or if fate didn't take a hand. She suddenly had a great feeling of danger. 'Anna, why are you going so fast?' She asked. 'There's no need to go so fast. Please, Anna, go slower!'

'I'm hardly doing anything at all, mama, but I'll go slower if you wish,' and she eased her foot off the accelerator.

'It's not as though we've got that far to go and I would like to arrive home safely. Accidents happen too easily.'

'Don't be nervous, mama. I'll get you home quite safely.' She turned to smile at her mother so obviously anxious and, turning back to look at the road ahead, in the headlights she suddenly saw him standing there. Her foot automatically slammed down hard on the brake. On the wet surface the car went into a violent uncontrollable skid before it overturned, rolling over and over, finally spinning like a teetotum on its bonnet before coming to a standstill.

In the virtual silence of the night, there was no sound but the rain drops sizzling on the hot undercarriage, the wheels were still turning but gradually came to a stop. There was no movement in the car.

The rain had stopped and the clouds parted for the moon to momentarily shine through before they obscured her again.

****

'Where is the girl now?' Giuseppe asked. He had had time to more or less sober up, having gone home, taken a large black coffee and, finally, something to eat as he was suddenly ravenous. There was some ancient cheese in the fridge so bread and cheese had to do. He was in the shower when the call came.

'Taken to the hospital', the doctor replied as he lit his second cigarette, 'I had to sedate her heavily, poor thing. I suppose the shock of seeing her husband collapse in front of her eyes was what possibly caused the miscarriage. Maybe if we had got to her sooner we might have been able to save the baby, but I guess we will never know.'

'And no one heard her scream?'

'Of course, the whole hotel heard her but, in a place like this, screams are usually nothing to worry about. They indicate something else entirely. You would think the other denizens...'

'Denizens?' Giuseppe raised an eyebrow. He was beginning to feel a bit squeamish and wished he hadn't eaten that bread and cheese.

'...would be out there,' he indicated the corridor, 'agog to find out what's going on, that's only human curiosity but, apart from the ambulance men and your policeman, the place would appear to be empty. That is both natural and unnatural. They just do not want to be seen or be involved if they can possibly avoid it. In the morning, or whenever, they will probably get all the news hot from the proprietor. You could try knocking on doors and asking questions but I doubt it would get you anywhere.'

'Hmn...' Giuseppe scratched beneath his chin. He hadn't shaved for a few days and his bristles there were starting to itch. He eyed the doctor's cigarette with some disgust and waved the smoke away from his face but the hint wasn't taken.

'What do you suppose made them stay in a dump like this in the first place? It's not your usual place for tourists to stay, well not newlyweds anyway, and judging by the clothes and possessions, they could very well have afforded something swankier. We do have better hotels. Maybe the boy would visit this one by himself in a few years down the line but certainly not with his wife.' This was said in all seriousness. It wasn't a time for joking. He gulped the last of his water from a plastic cup, screwed it up and tossed it into the waste bin on top of the stubs of two entry tickets to the museum. 'So what was the cause of death do you suppose?'

'An open and shut case by the looks of it, Giuseppe. From all the indications a heart attack.' The doctor gave a shrug. 'What's new about heart attacks? Happens all the time.' He took a deep draw on his cigarette.

'Heart attack! Then what the hell am I doing here?'

'The usual red tape and lots of it, just what the chief inspector likes to give you. By the way, when are you going to apologise?'

'When hell freezes over or when I see him riding up the via Torreone on a donkey with a carrot up his arse.'

'Well, in the meantime, this one is going to keep you filling in forms for a while. I'll let you have my report in the morning.' Despite the situation he couldn't help laughing as he picked up his black bag and headed for the bedroom door. He stopped and turned back for a moment.

'I'll let you know of the girl's condition as soon as there's any change. You'll want to speak to her no doubt.'

Giuseppe nodded and waved the doctor on his way. He looked down at the body on the floor. 'Poor sod,' he said then, to the police photographer, 'Have you finished?' The man didn't even bother to reply, just gave a nod and walked out of the room and Giuseppe shouted for the ambulance men patiently waiting outside and filling the passage with their own cigarette smoke. 'Don't you guys know you're not by law allowed to smoke in buildings anymore?' They ignored him. 'I could arrest you, you know that?' They still ignored him. 'Okay', he sighed, 'you can take him away now.' He sat down on the nearest chair and watched but not with much interest as the men lifted the corpse, placed it in a body bag, zipped it up, lowered it onto a stretcher and carried it out. Giuseppe looked around the room. "Why on earth were they staying in a dump like this?" he thought again. They must have been able to afford, not necessarily a five star, but at least a more up market one. He pushed himself out of the chair and went over to the wardrobe at the same time calling, 'Dino?'

His underling who had been standing guard outside the room appeared at the door and stood waiting for orders. It would seem Dino was another one who talked only if talk was absolutely necessary.

'The guy who runs this doss house, what's his name?'

'Fabrizio Botticello.'

'Where is he?'

'Downstairs I suppose.'

'Hmn…' He had gone to the wardrobe and was rummaging through pockets and finding them empty. He turned his attention to drawers and found what he wanted, a wallet holding money, traveller's cheques, credit cards, driving licence, all he needed for identification. Sometimes signatures in a hotel register weren't of much use and passports can be fakes. 'Bag everything and take it to the station,' he ordered as he started to go, 'and don't steal the hotel soap.'

'This hotel has soap?' Dino asked, raising his eyebrow in turn and flicking his cigarette butt into the waste bin. Giuseppe shook his head, not believing what he had just witnessed. 'Hey!' he yelled. 'You know you could start a fire if that thing isn't properly out?'

There was a shrug from the departing Dino. 'It's out,' he said, holding up his hand and rubbing his thumb and forefinger together and he disappeared ostensibly to collect bags. What had been nipped off had been trodden into the carpet. Dino was obviously a respecter of other people's property only if it was worth it. Giuseppe shook his head again and took a look in the bin to make absolutely sure the end was out and that was when he saw the two tickets. He took them out and stood surveying them for a while before slipping them in his pocket and leaving the room.

He felt dirty. He felt he wanted to get out of this place as fast as possible. He almost skipped down the stairs and, as he hurried across the lobby on his way out he was stopped by a yell from a gesticulating Fabrizio. The detective stopped and turned to face the reception desk for a moment.

'Who's going to pay their bill?' Fabrizio almost howled.

'Call the British Embassy', Giuseppe growled with some satisfaction as, smiling for the first time, rueful as it was, he left the Hotel Phoebe and went home to bed. As Scarlet O'Hara said, "Tomorrow is another day."

\*\*\*\*

Bunny was in a street market. There was a long row of stalls down one side. She was standing in front of one of them, a stall selling fruit. A religious procession approached and moved on by. Bunny stood watching, entranced. The Madonna carried shoulder high on her bier had a look of such sweet sadness. Bunny lowered her gaze from the statue to look at the penitents following. Two women in black, heads bowed, drew near and, when level with Bunny, turned their faces towards her. Bunny fell back in shock against the stall behind her. One of the women was Madam Rosetta; presumably the other was her daughter, Anna. The women had no eyes. Bunny clutched at something on the stall, what could it be? She looked down at her hand. She was holding a beating heart, the blood running through her fingers. It was her scream that woke her up.

\*\*\*\*

He hadn't been in his office more than two minutes when his intercom buzzed. 'Yes?' he said, fighting the urge to shout at whoever was on the other end.

'The chief inspector would like to see you in his office,' replied the silky voice of the chief's new secretary.

Anna Maria Macchi had somehow inveigled her way into the arms and the bed if not the heart of the chief inspector, as respectable a married man as respectable married men go and bored out of his mind with his wife and at continual odds with his children. If pushed he would admit not only to despairing but actively disliking the brats they had bred and couldn't wait to get shot of them. He knew for a fact they were always pulling rank – my father the chief of police – and there was not much he could do about it except yell at them time and time again.

Where, when, or how this turn of events with the delectable Macchi took place was still unknown to the station's gossips though there were any number of guesses, all probably far off the mark, but everyone knew of it when she turned up as his personal secretary and that had the gossips buzzing like flies over a warm wet cow pat.

Giuseppe climbed the stairs to the chief's office and politely knocked on the door, waiting a moment before entering. He would have been in even bigger trouble had he caught the chief in a compromising situation. Nobody in his position likes to be discovered with his pants around his ankles. It's so undignified for a start. Giuseppe, despite his own indulgence, always found himself laughing when he imagined people he knew having sex. Giuseppe had a pretty vivid imagination. It really was too ridiculous for words. He laughed when he watched simulated copulation in a movie. The men always seem to be doing it with their shoulders; that is, there was an awful lot of shoulder movement, forward, backwards, forward, backwards. He wondered if other people had noticed it. What the hell! Giuseppe thought, you don't fuck with your shoulders, you fuck with your hips. Why don't they get it right? Anyway, with the world absolutely awash with pornography, what was the point of these scenes anyway? They usually did no more than hold up the action. Maybe it was directors indulging in some sort of fantasy of their own and, if not laughable, they were usually very boring.

Maybe the director got his rocks off looking at the out-takes.

Anna Maria in the flesh lived up to the sexiness of her voice over the intercom, Giuseppe thought, surveying her appreciatively as she got up from behind her desk and, after knocking, opened the inner door to the chief's sanctum, and he wondered what that middle aged nonentity had that could have hooked and landed this particular exotic fish. Something came to mind but it didn't bear thinking about any more and was immediately dismissed.

'He's expecting you,' she breathed, looking remarkably like the young Lollabrigida even to the pout as she stood in the open doorway. There was no way Giuseppe without some difficulty could get passed her and her rather full chest she seemed to thrust out even further as he went by. Was she really trying to flirt with him? No doubt she flirted with every man she came across, he thought and, if that was the case, no doubt his original thought about the chief was spot on.

'Thank you,' he said and strode briskly into the room to face his chief sitting scowling like some pop-eyed malevolent toad behind his desk. It seemed to Giuseppe that he had never seen the chief without a scowl on his face and, new law or no new law, the office reeked of cigar smoke.

'That will be all, Miss Macchi,' the man growled before turning his baleful glare to Giuseppe. 'Now tell me, what's all this about some young tourist being found dead in one of the local knocking shops?'

Giuseppe didn't really hear the question at first. He was too inwardly amused by the "Miss Macchi" bit rather than "Anna" as though it pulled the wool over anybody's eyes, and it took a moment to sink in. It would seem also the chief was aware of the place and why not? He was after all the chief and really should be aware of everything happening in his neighbourhood. Probably where he first met Anna Maria, Giuseppe thought, or where they went anyway. He also thought he had better answer the question.

'Well to all intents and purposes, it would seem a natural death', he said. 'A heart attack, or so the doctor believes.'

'So young?'

'Heart attacks can happen any age, like ostensibly healthy young football players having never previously given any indication of anything wrong health-wise taking everyone by surprise suddenly dropping dead on the pitch.' He sniggered.

'What's so funny?'

'I was just thinking, if it was his kick that sent the ball flying into the back of the net and he passed out before actually seeing it, he would miss his own goal, and if it was a dive he was taking it would be the ultimate red card.'

'That's supposed to be funny?'

'Sorry.'

'You have a warped sense of humour, Borelli. We're talking about death here, no laughing matter. What about the wife?'

'The footballer's wife?'

'You're still trying to be funny? Because I really do not have time for your witticisms.'

"Witticisms," Giuseppe thought, "there's a big word for an ignoramus." 'It's only a sense of humour that keeps me going,' he said out loud, 'warped or not.' He was tempted for one moment to add he didn't think the wife had a sense of humour considering the circumstances but common sense stopped him in the nick of time. No, he thought, it wasn't funny, not funny at all. One of these days his imagination and his tongue were going to get him into really serious trouble even more so than when he opened it on that television programme. Baiting a bull is a dangerous occupation as he already knew to his cost.

'In stable condition in the hospital,' he said. 'Unfortunately it seems she lost the baby she was carrying. We're tracing the family through the embassy but that might take a little time I suppose. Unless the coroner's report indicates otherwise it looks like an open and shut case.'

'Well just make sure it stays that way.'

Giuseppe wondered, if the coroner's report indicated foul play, how he was going to keep it that way.

'We don't want any bad press over this thing,' the chief continued to make his meaning clear, as he took a cigar from a drawer and rolled it between his fingers, patting his pockets and looking around for matches. 'Local elections are coming up and a lot of people make a lot of money out of the tourist trade. It wouldn't do to have them staying away because of some mix up.' He found a box in another drawer and gave it a good shake just to make sure it still contained at least one match. Evidently it didn't and he tossed the box into the waste bin beneath his desk. 'On your way out ask Miss Macchi to get me some matches will you?'

Once again Giuseppe had to bite his tongue before pointing out the obvious that people are dying all the time whether the politicians approved of it or not and what sort of a mix up could there possibly be?

'And just make sure your report is typed up correctly, No mistakes. You're only on this because I can't spare anyone else. That's all, unless you have something else to say?' It was a hint that he would possibly and magnanimously let bygones be bygones if an apology was forthcoming but it wasn't.

'No, sir.' Giuseppe smiled and left the office. Once outside there was an even broader smile for Anna Maria and a decided wink to which it was her turn to raise an eyebrow.

'He's out of matches,' Giuseppe said.

****

Sergeant Ducati met a none too happy Giuseppe on the steps of the Critone museum. Sergeant Luka Ducati was one of those born smilers nature throws up every now and again. Sergeant Ducati seemed to smile all the time, even when none too happy or in pain. Sergeant Ducati walked, sat, lay down, ate his dinner, read a book, watched television, talked to his wife and his fellow police officers or members of the public with a permanent smile on his face. He more than likely even smiled in his sleep and one day would be smiling in his coffin and it wouldn't be rictus. Sometimes people found Ducati's smile charming, uplifting even, sometimes his smile was truly unnerving, especially to miscreants who thought it meant he had some hidden knowledge up his sleeve or about to indulge in some none too politically correct behaviour. He was smiling now as he greeted Giuseppe with a bright "good morning" even though he could see Giuseppe was in a thoroughly bad mood.

'What's so good about it?' is what he got in return. 'I have a body in the morgue, a poor bereaved hysterical young lady in the hospital, a dead baby, a psychic who warned me all this would happen and who I took no notice of and who I can't find now to maybe clarify matters further. Not, mind you, that I believe in any of that nonsense but one never knows. There are more things in heaven and earth.'

'What does that mean?'

'It's a quotation.'

'Oh? But what's it supposed to mean?'

'It means when you drop your bread on the carpet it always lands butter down. Now, if you don't mind, and even though I love this chit-chat, can we get on with what we're supposed to be doing? Last night I missed her by that much.' He held up his hand, thumb and forefinger together.

'Who?'

'The psychic. She drove past me in her car. And on top of it all, I am burdened with a chief inspector who is a complete arsehole which I suppose is one up on being half an arsehole.'

Throughout this mini tirade Ducati never stopped smiling which only irked Giuseppe more even though he was fully aware it was the man's nature or mannerism. Maybe his smiler gene was simply overpowering and like a runaway vehicle on a steep hill just couldn't be controlled.

'Something interesting to do today then?' Ducati's smile if possible was even broader as he indulged in a little good-hearted goading.

By this time they were through the doors and heading for the information desk when Giuseppe stopped, turned, and performed a good imitation of the chief's scowl towards his smiling sergeant.

'No, Sergeant, the same old thing, you know, traffic tickets, traffic tickets, and more traffic tickets and, oh, if you're really in luck, I might just let you type up this report for me and I know how you enjoy doing that one chubby finger at a time. Now let's ask a few questions for that lovely report the chief's so eager to get his hands on, shall we?' He was tempted to give the sergeant a pat on the cheek but resisted it as he turned once more and faced the desk behind which the gum-chewing young lady sat waiting to issue him with a ticket of admission or not as the case might be. Sometimes people got as far as the foyer, took a look around and left. She was already clutching her little book in one hand, ready to tear out the tickets with the fingers of the other. It had obviously been a dull morning and she had forgotten to bring in her magazine. Nevertheless she greeted the pair with a scowl as though they were unwanted guests come to overstay their welcome.

'Is the curator here?' Giuseppe asked, completing his walk to the desk.

'No,' the girl replied through her gum chewing. 'Gone to the library. Spends more time in there than in here if you asks me.'

'Then you may be able to help,' he said, flashing his identity card of which she took hardly any notice and it certainly didn't stop her chewing. If anything the jaw movement was increased, though that could have been the sign of a nervous reaction. People do tend to react nervously when faced with the police even though they may be totally innocent of any wrong doing.

'I'm Inspector Borelli and this big grinning object standing next to me is Sergeant Ducati.'

Ducati duly gave her one of his broadest smiles. Giuseppe regarded him for a moment, shook his head, and turned back to the girl behind the desk. 'Your name is?'

'Dalila.'

'Well, Dalila, I was wondering if you happened to see a couple of English tourists who may have been in here sometime yesterday, a young couple.'

Dalila shrugged.

'Maybe you would remember the wife was pregnant.'

'Oh, them. Yeh, I saw them.' She chewed for a minute as though she was thinking of what to say next and was then distracted by an elderly couple wanting to pay for admittance. They seemed to be rather impatient, the man clearing his throat rather loudly to get attention. She ripped off the tickets with a nonchalance that equalled Ducati's smile and handed them over in exchange for the notes that she inspected as though they might possibly be forgeries and for which she would be held accountable. Giuseppe patiently waited. She put the notes away in the till drawer beneath the desk and continued as if there had been no interruption. 'Germans,' she whispered loud enough for the departing couple to hear.

'No, English,' Giuseppe contradicted her.

'No, Germans,' she contradicted him in turn. 'Those two.' She inclined her head towards the couple just disappearing into the nearest gallery. 'Always in a hurry they are, Germans, never a please or a thank you but just get on and do your job. They'll whip around the museum in ten minutes flat you watch and think they've seen everything. They're like that. You can always tell if someone's German. Humph.'

'The English couple,' Giuseppe prompted.

'Oh, yeh. In a right old state he was, I can tell you.'

'What do you mean?'

'Like he was in a sort of shock like, you know, sweating all over, clutching his chest.' She clutched at her own to emphasize it.

'You mean he had a heart attack?' Ducati asked, still smiling incongruously.

'Oh, I never thought of that,' she said, smiling in turn and giving the side of her neck a scratch. 'How would I know anyway? Yeh, maybe that's what it was, though I wouldn't know now, would I?' On removal she looked at her fingernail with some interest in case any of her neck had come away with it. Satisfied none of it had she gave the nail a quick flick and waited for a further question.

It wasn't forthcoming because Giuseppe was irritated by the reiteration but silently counted to ten as the girl continued. 'Do you reckon on it being that? I was working the cafeteria at the time, that's my main job here, and he kept going on about it being evil or something like that. My English was never very good at school though I've had to learn a bit more in this job of course, never learnt German though which doesn't really matter because if they don't speak Italian they understand English but I thought maybe he was talking about the pain, you know?' She kept giving Ducati sideways glances wondering why he was still smiling. It was totally weird she thought. Maybe there was something wrong with him, but should he be a policeman if that was the case? Well, it was no business of hers; whatever he was smiling at was his affair. It takes all kinds, even in the police force.

'Did he say anything else?'

'Not that I remember, but she did. "Here, drink this," she said or something like that, meaning a glass of water, and I made them two strong black coffees. I nearly spoiled that order by adding milk but she stopped me just in time, then, "We'll go back to the hotel," she said, "we've had enough adventures for one day." I understood that. She could see he was looking pretty bad. I remember wondering if they would make it but then I thought maybe they would be staying close by, almost around the corner as it were, so it would be all right, you know.' Dalila had probably never before strung so many words together and had for a while forgotten to chew but that was now renewed with extra vigour.

'And what do you suppose she meant by that?' Giuseppe asked.

'Meant by what?'

'About having had enough adventures for one day.'

'Why ask me. You're the cops, aren't you?' She said as she chewed with renewed vigour and blew a bubble.

'Was there anyone else in the museum while they were here?'

'Of course. There's attendants aren't there? To keep a watch on what people might get up to in the galleries. You never know with people, do you? Some of them can be totally weird. I sometimes work all hours, you know, gets me some extra money for the baby.'

'Baby?'

'Yeh. Spends most of her time with my mother, but I like to give her a little something every now and again, you know, like a proper mother should.'

'Yes, quite,' replied Giuseppe with only the faintest idea what this garrulous girl was going on about. 'So you must have locked up after they left.'

'Me? No.' She blew another bubble, bigger than the first and with her little finger nail scraped the remains off her chin before she continued. Giuseppe was beginning to lose patience. 'That Francesco would have done that. In fact he was here as well, wasn't he? I'd forgotten all about him.'

'And who exactly is Francesco?'

'Caretaker, isn't he? He's always here. Been here since he was a kid if you ask me. I sometimes wonder he doesn't sleep here. His father was caretaker here before him, sort of keeping it in the family as it were. If you see him he'll tell you how Mussolini talked to his father and patted him on the shoulder. He tells everybody that. He'll also tell you how his father gave Mussolini the evil eye and that's why that man came to a bad end. That was terrible wasn't it? I've seen pictures, him and his lady love hanging upside down from lampposts. Terrible.' She shook her head in disbelief. Giuseppe wondered she did not cross herself but then maybe like him she was not of a religious bent.

Ducati had obviously decided this line of questioning was getting nowhere and decide to put in his pennyworth once more.

'And whereabouts would he have been when the Englishman was having his heart attack?'

'Who?'

Giuseppe raised a supercilious eyebrow in Ducati's direction and received a smile in return.

'The caretaker.'

'Well, I was in the cafeteria, wasn't I? So he could have been here at the desk I suppose to take their money. There's another girl supposed to do that but she's off sick which is why I'm here today. Cafeteria's closed for the moment. Dead mean they are as far as staff's concerned.'

'You mean he was having a heart attack when he came in?'

'Who? Oh, you mean the Englishman. No. That is, not that I know of. No, couldn't have been because they had a good look around, ages they were, and I know that because of what the curator said when she saw them downstairs.'

'Downstairs?'

The girl looked at Giuseppe as if he was thickest policeman who ever walked.

'In the cafeteria,' she said with definite emphasis on the second to last syllable. 'That's where I saw them wasn't it?' She gave her head a shake indicating she thought she might be dealing with idiots here.

'And what did the curator say?'

'Can't remember now but it must have been something to do with them looking around, mustn't it?'

It was at this point that Giuseppe gave up. 'Well, when will the curator be back?'

The girl shrugged.

'Do you mind if the sergeant takes a look around?'

'No skin off my nose.'

'And when you see him would you tell the curator I would like to have words with him.'

'Her.'

'Her?'

'Yes, her. She's a she.'

'New is she?' This was from Ducati. The girl nodded.

'Very well, words with her. She can telephone me at the station when she's free to talk.' He turned to Sergeant Ducati. 'In the meantime, you take a look around.'

'What for?'

'Because I say so that's what for. Ask this Francesco a few questions and any attendant you come across, though I doubt you will get any answers. Don't forget the chief wants a report in triplicate so let's make sure we've got something to tell him. I'll see you back at the station.'

He was already heading towards the main door.

'She's feeling a bit off-colour this morning, if you ask me, the curator.'

Giuseppe stopped and turned around. 'Why is that do you suppose?'

The girl shrugged. 'I don't know, do I? She didn't say anything. I just guessed.'

She blew another bubble and this time scraped it off her upper lip.

Giuseppe turned away once more.

'What's he been up to then, this English person?'

This time Giuseppe didn't even bother to turn around. 'He hasn't been up to anything. He's dead.'

For a moment she stropped chewing as she hastily crossed herself.

\*\*\*\*

A weary, disgruntled, frustrated Giuseppe with a throbbing headache and aching feet sat in Umberto's café toying with the glass that held his grappa and inwardly cursing his choice of profession. He desperately, when young, had dreams of being a footballer with all the fame and glamour that went with it and, if he could have been snapped up by an English club, all that money, but he simply didn't have the talent. If he kicked a ball he was quite likely to lose his balance and fall over let alone send it flying towards the goal. He wished he had a home to go back to, a real home that is and not his pokey little joint that was the last word in inhospitable disorganised discomfort. Maybe one of these days he might be able to afford something better, something with a more hygienic bathroom for starters. Giuseppe was a great one for personal hygiene, particularly in the summer, and his bathroom gave him the shudders every time he used it. No amount of scrubbing, no amount of bleach was going to get rid of the ring around the bath or the stains in the bowl. Okay, maybe it was the water, but the stains were unsightly nevertheless.

He couldn't go back to living with mama, his beautiful mama, because Syracuse was far too far away to commute from and these days socks were no longer darned. They were so cheap, probably imported from China or some other Oriental country employing slave labour in sordid sweat shops, it was simpler to go out and buy more. He'd heard all about those establishments and the piracy of big brand names but if people could buy cheap they would buy cheap, there was no gainsaying that, and he also knew about the skin trade, much of which was closer to home, and that was something that really upset him.

If he weren't stationed where he was he felt he might have been a member of Interpol and be in a position to do something about it. Anyway, as far as socks were concerned, you just went out and bought new ones. Well she might not, like a good mama, darn his socks anymore as she did when he was a child but she still had her lace to keep her occupied and her neighbours to socialise with so she was all right. He did miss her food sometimes, there's nothing like home cooking, though there was always Arturo and Maria to fall back on. Maybe he should ask for a transfer, but to where? Sometimes he missed his old home town. The friends he grew up with were all still there. Who did he have here? Sergeant Luka Ducati who had a wife and bambini and his own life to lead. There were times Giuseppe really felt lonely and sorry for himself. One of these days, he thought, he would really have to ask some nice lady to marry him.

He looked across at the men concentrating as always on their game of cards. What else did they have to do? In between sleeping and eating whatever their wives dished up, played their interminable games in Umberto's café, making a drink or a coffee last a long time? Giuseppe wondered how on earth Umberto made a living his customers ordered so little and his charges being far from exorbitant; but then maybe he had something else up his sleeve that no one knew about, that nobody was supposed to know about. He wouldn't be the only one. But why speculate on that when he had enough problems trying to sort out the young Englishman's strange death, because he still believed there was something unnatural about it no matter what the doctor said.

Alceste was in his usual place with his glass of prickly pear liqueur and the day's newspaper on the table in front of him. Every now and again he would sniff loudly as though something in the paper struck him as being slightly improper. As far as he was concerned the world, as the Americans would say, was going to hell in a hand basket and the pace of its descent was quickening by the day. Those whom the gods wished to destroy they first make mad. After a while he sensed Giuseppe was regarding him with some interest and he looked up from the paper and nodded, took a final sip of his liqueur, looked into the glass to ensure he had taken the last drop and, carrying the paper, advanced on Giuseppe's table prior presumably to leaving.

Beniamino had just finished the aria from Tosca that international football and a famous tenor, later three tenors, had made famous but the record was still turning and the needle having scratched its way to the end was now going click click click click before Umberto got up from the card table to lift the head and place the arm in its clip. Flat handed he stopped the record from turning, while with the other hand winding up, though he obviously had no intention of playing another at the moment. Having wound the machine to its fullest extent, he had to be careful not to over wind it, he could cause some irrevocable damage, he returned to his game.

Meantime an argument had broken out at the card table and although it was unlikely that blood would be shed, it grew in intensity, gesticulation and volume until Umberto yelled out that he had had enough, turned on his heels and went back to put Gigli on the gramophone again to calm things down a bit. The men having evidently settled whatever the bone of contention was in the previous game, a new hand was now being dealt. There would no doubt be silence while the players concentrated on studying their cards and made life and death decisions. Giuseppe told himself that if he didn't forget it, the next time he came by he would bring them a couple of new packs. Some of these were so damaged it was pretty obvious from the marks on their backs what they were and that no doubt was what started the row. It was like playing with loaded dice.

Alceste had stopped by Giuseppe's table, obviously fascinated by the goings on at the card table even though it was a pretty regular occurrence. Now he turned his attention to Giuseppe. 'Well, Mister Policeman, found your Madam Rosetta yet?' he asked, or rather cackled, grinning and showing his tooth.

Giuseppe raised an eyebrow. 'Why do you ask that? If I remember, correct me if I'm wrong, old man, you said I wouldn't find her but she would come to me. Changed your mind have you?'

Alceste shook his head. 'But she has come to you,' he said.

'What do you mean by that?'

Alceste laid the paper on the table and pointed with a bony finger. 'There she is,' he said which only went to prove that he could actually see to read.

Giuseppe looked at the photograph of the upturned car, a Fiat, and the report that went with it and his outlook on life was suddenly even gloomier than before. 'Umberto,' he called, 'bring me another drink.'

# CHAPTER 6

Arms folded in an unmistakable piece of body language that could spell trouble for someone, Bunny stood at the edge of the square watching the dig's progress. Everyone had greeted her warmly and stopped to wave or say a few words and Vincenzo had pulled himself out of his particular section to trot over and say more than a brief hello. Of that little shit Salvatore there was no sign. "Must have seen me coming," Bunny thought. "Never mind, sooner or later he will have to resurface and then I'll give him a piece of my mind. What more can I do? I don't want to be had up on a murder charge, do I? I could plead temporary insanity."

'I think we found most of the interesting stuff before you left,' Vincenzo said. 'It's really just bits and pieces now, you know, shards of pottery and that.'

'Is that meant to comfort me?' She glowered in the direction of Enrico Agostino who had as yet not noticed or at least acknowledged her presence and, if looks could kill, he would have dropped dead on the spot.

'What's he like?' She nodded in Agostino's direction. 'No, don't tell me. I don't want to know. Can't think why I asked it in the first place.'

It was quite obvious that the little green-eyed monster was gnawing away and Bunny would probably be the first to admit it, if only to herself.

'Except for one particular object,' Vincenzo continued.

'Oh? And what was that?' Curiosity was piqued.

'Hmn…' Vincenzo scratched his nose with a grubby finger. He was going to stretch this one out and she knew it. She laughed and gave him a dig in the ribs which almost doubled him up.

'Come on, Vincenzo, don't keep me in suspense.'

'A kernos. At least that is what he called it.'

His timing was perfect. He waited for her reaction and, after a lengthy pause, he got it.

'Bronze Age, Mycenaean! Where is it? Show it to me!' She was almost breathless with excitement.

'It's in Rome.'

There was a long silence.

'What did you say?'

'I said, it's in Rome.'

There was an even longer silence as she stared at him almost stupefied, and then it really looked as if she would burst into tears.

'I'm sorry, Bunny. Whether it's of Mister Bighead's making,' now he tilted his head in Agostino's direction, 'or whether it was an order from up above, everything is going back to Rome. What's already in the museum here, all the earlier discoveries, they have magnanimously agreed to let stay for a while for the benefit of the locals and the town. The mayor of course is over the moon at all the publicity. You would think we were the centre of the universe.'

'You've taken photographs of course.'

'Of course.'

'May I see?'

'Copies of all the photographs are being given to you. If the museum can't have the real thing then at least people can see what has been dug up and what their museum has been robbed of.'

'A kernos,' Bunny said. 'I can't believe it.'

'That's what the man called it. A strange looking object I have to say. I've never seen anything like it before.'

'I have. There's one in the Vathy Museum on Samos. I don't recall there being any others. It's 7th Century BC which makes our previous finds here even older than I thought.'

Eventually Agostino would have to acknowledge Bunny's presence, if just to make sure Vincenzo wasn't putting the boot in, and he did so now, giving her a smile and a little wave. He made no attempt to move closer though and, in fact, indicated to Vincenzo that he ought to be back on the job. Without acknowledging the man's greeting, Bunny turned on her heel and left. After all he had made no previous attempt to call on her and he had every opportunity to do so, and the news that everything was to be shipped back to Rome really stuck in her gizzard; but she couldn't wait to see the photographs, especially of the kernos. That just had to be the most exciting find yet.

As a little girl her parents had instilled into her the belief that she should never ever think evil of anyone or wish them hurt and it would take more than ten Hail Mary's and four Our Father's to put things right. Maybe Agostino was actually a very nice person. On the other hand, maybe he wasn't. It was not that she resented the fame, the honours, and all that went with it when something completely unique was found, it was simply that she loved her work: tedious, dirty, and backbreaking though it sometimes was; the delving into the distant past and making those discoveries was reward enough. So she wasn't going to wish Agostino might slip into a trench and break a leg or anything like that. No, she had lost out so she might as well let him get on with it. Still she couldn't but help that insidious feeling of jealousy and she would have to put a stop to it before real damage was done. No doubt he would reap his just deserts, his karma, sooner or later. She would leave it to the fates, whatever they had in store for him. When she was small she was bullied mercilessly by her brother until one day, when tears and pleading were not enough to stop him, she lashed out and caught him full in the face with a little clenched fist. The sight of the blood streaming from his nose gave her a momentary fright that gave vent to an ear-splitting scream, the kind of scream only small girls can make, both in pitch and decibels; but also, once that passed, a feeling of intense satisfaction. He never bullied her again and that, she thought, was how to treat men, well how to treat bullies anyway. Give them a taste of their own medicine.

\*\*\*\*

'Have you heard about Sergeant Ducati?' The man on the desk asked as Giuseppe walked or rather schlepped into the station.

'No? What about Ducati?'

Giuseppe had had a very disturbed night, called out no fewer than three times for emergency domestics none of which turned out to be an emergency, on top of which he had spent the earlier part of the evening in Umberto's. He was half asleep, had a splitting headache and in no mood for anything. He just wished he wouldn't let this job frustrate him so much. Could it be he took it far too seriously? But what would be the point of being a policeman otherwise?

'He's in the hospital, suspected heart attack.'

Giuseppe was instantly wide awake and he shivered violently. This was unbelievable, it was too macabre.

'You all right?'

'Yes, yes. I'm all right. If anyone wants me I'm at the hospital, okay?' And Giuseppe turned and went straight out again almost at a run. He simply couldn't believe this was on the cards. Ducati was a fitness freak. He didn't smoke, He didn't drink. He religiously took his exercise. He drank eight glasses of water a day and ate five portions of fruit. He firmly believed sex more than once a week was unhealthy, debilitating if nothing else and was totally faithful to his wife who he adored, as she did him. In fact he had propagated that sexual theory in the station so became known as "The once a week man". Maybe that was why he was smiling all the time, waiting in expectation for the week to pass. Surely there was simply no way someone like this should have had a heart attack.

In his car, Giuseppe turned on the ignition and turned it off again. He sat for a while realising he was trembling quite violently and really in no fit state to drive. He took deep breaths and, when he had calmed down somewhat and felt up to it, he switched on the ignition again, put the car in gear and drove off, trying to keep his mind from the most morbid of thoughts, the most morbid of which was what if he arrived too late?

At the hospital he was directed to where Ducati lay; the single occupant in a small room. When Giuseppe arrived he found the sergeant's wife, Rosina, seated at his bedside holding his hand.

Giuseppe gave her a nod which she returned and then, at the bedside, he took Ducati's other hand and held it before he leaned forward and kissed him. Then he pulled up a chair and seated himself. He couldn't believe it; Ducati was as white as a sheet and still smiling.

'You bastard!' he said. 'You bastard!' He found himself trembling again, this time, from the emotion of the moment, the tears welling up. 'What is the meaning of this? What're you playing at? You can lie there smiling. You're skiving, that's what you're doing. You're...' He wanted to swear but in time remembered Rosina's presence. The tears now were running down his cheeks and he had to take out his handkerchief and wipe them away. Rosina smiled at him, understanding, but said nothing. She was still clutching her husband's hand and now she gave him a smile as well and Giuseppe, seeing it, relaxed a little.

'So, okay, tell me all about it then. That's if you're up to it.'

'I'm up to it. It's not as bad as it might have been.'

'So what happened? What do the doctors say? What's the prognosis?'

'A few days complete rest and, as you can see, they've got me wired up.'

'See? See? I said you were skiving. Now, if Rosina doesn't mind, tell me how all this came about.' He lifted both hands in the air as though he just couldn't believe this.

'I was in the museum. I went back to have a word or two with Bunny.'

'Bunny? Who the hell is bunny? Sorry Rosina.'

'The curator. That's what they call her, Bunny.'

'Yes, okay, and?'

'I was sort of wandering around, you know, just curious. Believe it or not I'd never been in there before, was never that interested, not even as a kid, and I was waiting for her, in this room where they've put all the stuff they found in the square, when I saw this little lad.'

Once again Giuseppe felt himself go cold and that shiver ran up his back, the same kind of shiver when as a kid he was told ghost stories and he believed them.

'Are you all right, Giuseppe?' Rosina asked, frowning, 'you look very pale.'

'I'm all right.' He nodded. 'Go on.'

'Well, I thought the lad looked a bit strange, you know. He was wearing something that looked like old Romans or Greeks used to wear but he was a very handsome child, I would even go so far as to say beautiful, you can say that about a boy can't you? And he was smiling. I remember his eyes. His eyes were so bright, so bright, a bright blue.' Ducati stopped and closed his own eyes.

'Do you want something?' Rosina asked, looking more than a little concerned. 'Shall I call the nurse?'

She stood up to stretch out for the bell when he shook his head so she sat down again still looking worried and glanced across the bed at Giuseppe, a look that said maybe this was not such a good time for questions, but Giuseppe decided to ignore it. After a moment Ducati opened his eyes and Giuseppe waited, deciding though not to push it.

'He put out his little arms like he wanted to come to me or me to go to him, I remember they were so skinny, his arms, almost like matchsticks but then children that age can be awfully thin can't they? And that's when all of a sudden, when he put out his arms, that's when I felt this tightness in my chest. Then the pain started. I heard Bunny's voice. She must have come into the room at that very moment but I must have passed out because the next thing I knew I was lying here in this bed.'

Giuseppe really didn't know what to say. First of all Antonio, then the Englishman, and did this hallucination, this apparition, because that is what it must surely be, have anything to do with the deaths of Madam Rosetta and her daughter? And now Ducati. He was certain that if the curator hadn't walked in on him at that moment and... and what? Broken the spell? Ducati would be a dead man. No, no no! It was all nonsense. Witches and spells and strange gods disappeared a long long time ago and he refused to believe any of this; though he would definitely be asking a few more questions but where to start? Well, obviously Bunny would appear to be the answer to that.

He got to his feet. 'Ciao Rosina.' And then to Ducati, 'We'll talk later,' he said. 'In the meantime get well and...' he winked and pointed his index finger at him, thumb in the air, pretended gun fashion '... keep smiling.'

****

Bunny and Vincenzo were in her office keenly examining the photographs of the kernos pinned up on a board together with pictures of various other finds including the boys' heads. She was bitterly disappointed that she hadn't been given the opportunity of examining the kernos in reality before it was shipped off.

'What do you suppose it was for?' Vincenzo asked, and then, so as not to appear a complete ignoramus, 'I mean, I have a pretty good idea but maybe you could fill me in in more detail.'

The kernos was an earthenware ring about thirty centimetres in diameter decorated with three fairly large cups positioned at intervals and interspersed with odd figures; a pomegranate, a bull's head, a lion's head and a frog. It was in almost perfect condition, just a minor chip on the rim of one of the cups.

'Well quite obviously, looking at the three cups, it was for votive offerings. What the weird motley of figures represents I have no idea but it is presumed they were symbolic or for ritual reasons. I must assume ancient Greek religion was extremely complex.'

'It's definitely Greek then.'

'Oh, yes. No doubt about it.'

For a while they gazed at a photograph in silence before moving on to another. Bunny shook her head.

'I wonder', she said, 'if there is any connection between this and our two boys.' She cast a glance in the direction of their photographs. She couldn't think of them other than her two boys. 'Ah, well, best get on. Thank you for bringing these, Vincenzo. Will you be going back to the dig now?'

'Of course. Any message for Mister Bighead?' He grinned, but Bunny was not amused.

'You don't have to give him a message', she said, 'he's standing right behind you.'

Vincenzo froze as his balls turned cold and then slowly turned around to see his boss, a smiling Agostino standing in the doorway. He would like to have said something, made an apology perhaps, it was only a joke but, just as his testicles had shrivelled, his tongue had done the opposite and suddenly seemed to be three times larger than normal.

'Good morning to you both,' Agostino greeted them, never losing the smile.

Bunny wanted to say, "Is it? And it's got even worse with your appearance." Instead she merely stared at the man not trusting herself to say something she would later regret.

'Professa, I would like to say...' He looked at Vincenzo. 'Shouldn't you be at the dig?'

'Yes, yes. I was just going. I brought these photographs around for the Professoressa. She was really anxious to see them.'

'Of course. Well, you've done your good deed for the day so it's back to work, is it not?'

Vincenzo's tongue had returned to its normal size but he had to, like Bunny, figuratively speaking, bite it in order not to say anything untoward. He merely made a slight bow, gave a 'Good-day, Professa,' and left with his dignity intact. Unfortunately that didn't last as, in his haste to get away, he tripped over his own feet and nearly went sprawling. He looked back and grinned. Bunny smiled. The ice wasn't broken but it was cracked.

'Can we talk?'

Bunny shrugged. What was there to talk about? He had muscled in on her job, pushed her aside, and now what did he want from her? To make amends? To make friends? There was something eerie about this man. She couldn't put a finger on what it might be; she simply would not or could not trust him. Maybe it was that ridiculous moustache. Maybe it was his eyes that never seemed to really focus on you as he talked. There was no denying he was a very handsome man but she had the feeling, ridiculous as it might seem, that if she touched him she would find his skin to be ice-cold.

He took his pipe from a jacket pocket and looked around for somewhere to empty it.

'Even if the new law hadn't come in,' Bunny said, 'a museum is hardly the place to smoke.' She knew this sounded petty but it was probably the tiniest of victories and any victory no matter how small made her feel better.

Without a word he returned the pipe to his pocket and there was a hiatus as he looked around the room. Whatever he had to say he was obviously finding it difficult to start and maybe the pipe would have helped. Bunny certainly wasn't going to. She folded her arms and waited; a second small victory. He got the message.

'Professa, I know you believe you've been treated rather badly.'

Bunny snorted. It wasn't exactly ladylike but it was all she could manage to show her feelings. She was just glad her nose wasn't running. That would have been most infra dig.

'Would you object if I sat down?'

Bunny extended an arm and an open hand towards a chair and Agostino sat.

'Let me explain the situation please.'

Bunny sat behind her desk, anticipating a load of flannel, and the look on her face, which he couldn't fail to notice, said as much.

****

Giuseppe was a worried man. He had been sitting in front of the computer for what seemed an age surfing the internet and discovering there were over six hundred thousand entries for lunar cults including examples mentioned in the Old Testament.

Mesopotamia, Syria, Egypt, they all had their moon goddesses. Egypt was most interesting because animals that were the embodiment of Thoth and Ibis in temples of Isis were found in Italy, arriving presumably via Greece. One site had no fewer than nine moon cults listed. From Pagan times around ten thousand BC, that is in the Palaeolithic age, the moon was a goddess all powerful and certainly never to be taken lightly and women were the guardians of her power.

Of course, sooner or later, men as is their wont, had to horn in and turn goddesses into priestesses and gods into priests. Thoth became a moon god, which information brought Giuseppe back from Egypt via Greece to Italy.

He sighed, closed down, and sat back, thinking. He was no nearer to understanding what it was all about than when he started. The lunar cults were no doubt continued with witchcraft. Witches and warlocks or wizards still existed casting their spells and he was certain that Madam Rosetta was a witch. How effective the spells were and how much was in the mind he really had no idea.

The morning was well advanced and he was stiff from sitting so long and felt in dire need of a drink so decided he would call in on Ducati first and find out how he was getting on before retiring to Umberto's café for an aperitif, after which it would be lunch time and he would go around to his cousin's trattoria for something to eat. He felt his appetite had returned.

****

'It was not I who had you removed from the dig, please believe me. The decision had already been taken before I was called in. I wasn't even consulted. In fact, I tried to have it overturned though I didn't think you would be all that pleased to be nominated as my assistant so maybe I didn't try hard enough, for which I am sorry, but second best I know is not in your nature.'

'You know?'

'Very well, I suspected. Am I right?'

Bunny shrugged and looked down as she toyed with a pencil on her desk. She had decided she would listen and she was listening even if eventually she didn't believe a word of it.

'So I suggested, I admit this and I had my reasons, I suggested you for this occupancy at the museum.'

'You had reasons?' She looked up at him.

'Indeed.'

She had to admit his smile when he turned it on was most becoming. He was certainly not lacking in charm but there was still something disconcerting about it and she squirmed a little and put down the pencil, wanting now to concentrate as hard as possible on this man she had considered her bete noir from the beginning.

'Your reasons.'

'I wanted to keep you close by so that, if necessary, I could pick your brains.' He laughed, seemingly a little embarrassed by this confession.

'You wanted to pick my brains.' She laughed in turn. 'I am truly sorry, Doctor, but I simply do not believe that.'

It was his turn to shrug.

'But it's true. You are more of an expert on ancient Greece than I and I honestly thought we could work together. There have been exciting discoveries I am sure you agree and I am also sure there is more, much more to come. This dig could change the whole way we think of the Early Greeks in Italy. After all, we're only half way through. There's some way to go yet and I am sure much more to discover. When I publish the results I will make absolutely certain you get your fair share of the credit.'

"Boy oh boy!" Bunny thought, "is this guy a regular smoothie or isn't he?" And she couldn't help genuinely smiling for the first time.

'All right then, tell me this, why was I removed in the first place, presuming you're telling the truth and you had nothing to do with it?'

'I was never informed of the reason.' He shrugged again and shook his head.

'There you are then. It was all cut and dried before you appeared on the scene? Before you were called in? How did they know you would accept? What happened to your excavations in Egypt? I've read about them. They were pretty far advanced. How could you just abandon them at a moment's notice? I'm sorry but I can't help feeling there is something more to all this, something that doesn't quite meet the eye, doesn't add up.'

'You think in this case two and two make five, huh?'

Bunny felt the goose bumps rise. The Pentacle, the five pointed star sacred to Isis, to paganism and magic!

'Yes', she said weakly, 'something like that, even five and a half maybe.'

****

Giuseppe had made his way to the hospital with the sole purpose of seeing Ducati but he decided, if the girl was up to it, he might as well while he was there, kill two birds as it were.

The doctor said he didn't want to perform an autopsy on Richard if it could be avoided. "Don't want to send him back home sliced up from sternum to pubes, do we?" He said through his cigarette smoke and, if it were a natural death, there would be no need for one despite his youth; but Giuseppe had to try and ascertain exactly what went on in that room that night before a final decision could be made.

He found Ducati was up and about and still smiling, itching to be on his way, but evidently the doctors thought it advisable he stay for another couple of days, so Giuseppe backed them up. 'Better safe than sorry,' he said and, despite his disappointment, Ducati gave in and never lost his smile. Giuseppe couldn't understand it. It was uncanny, unnatural but then, as Goethe once remarked, how can you call anything in nature unnatural?

So, having made polite enquiries regarding the family, he left Ducati and, after ascertaining the whereabouts of Charmaine, made his way to the ward where she lay, evidently up to being questioned.

She was lying on her back with her eyes closed and, at first, he thought she was asleep but, after a while, she opened them and looked at him standing at the foot of the bed. He smiled at her but got no reaction. Her eyes were of the palest blue and reminded him of someone or something though he couldn't think what. The time had come for him to show his mastery of the English language. He had worked hard on it all his life and was very proud of being totally bilingual, or so he thought. Had he been put to the test in French or German he would have been at a complete loss.

'Good morning...' He looked down at her chart and up again '...Mrs Cummings. I am Inspector Borelli and, if you can stand for it, I must ask you a few questions. First may I give you my sympathies at the tragic decease of your husband and child but this interview is I am afraid of a necessity.'

She lay looking at him for a long while before she spoke. 'Where is Richard?' she whispered as though she hadn't heard him.

'Excuse me?'

'Where is Richard? My husband. Where is he?'

Did she not remember that her husband was dead? To tell her that he was lying in a fridge would have been too cruel so, to put it in his own words, for a moment he was on the horns of a dilemma. He moved to the side of the bed and pulled up a chair while he thought of what he was going to say next.

'Do you not recall what happened, Mrs Cummings?'

'Yes I do, of course I do, but where is Richard now?'

There was nothing for it but to be blunt. 'He is, I am sorry to say this to you, in the mortuary, Mrs Cummings, waiting to be shipped back to England just so quickly as we can finally sort out what happened that night to make sure there were no suspicious circumstances, that no foul play was involved.'

'Foul play? How could there have been foul play? What are you talking about? I don't understand.'

'If you will answer my questions you will come to understand.'

There was another silence as she lay regarding him and he wasn't eager to push her. Gently gently would be the order of the day. He finally decided to break the silence. 'Will you permit it?'

She gave a nod and he could see she was trying desperately to hold back the tears.

'Maybe it would be best if you started to tell me exactly what you remember about what happened that night and, if I need to ask you something, I will stop you. Is that all right?'

Again she nodded and lay there thinking for a while.

'Perhaps you would like a glass of water?' He reached out for the carafe on the bedside cabinet with the thick glass tumbler upside down on the neck but she shook her head.

'I don't know what time it was,' she whispered. He leaned closer in order to hear. 'We had been asleep you see. Yes, it must have been very late. Well gone midnight. Then I woke up because all of a sudden the baby made itself felt. I knew it had started, the birth I mean, and I woke Richard. After that it is all a bit of a blur. He was up and getting dressed, yes, I seem to remember he couldn't find his trousers and then suddenly, suddenly, I think this is how it happened, he just fell to the floor. I remember I was screaming. I was screaming not just because of Richard but because of the pain and the baby started to appear. That's when I must have passed out.'

'I see. Did you try and reach out for your husband at all?'

She shook her head. 'I don't remember if I did that. Who was it found us?' She asked.

'The hotel proprietor. He says your screams woke him up and he was so worried he decided to investigate. The bedroom door was locked but naturally he has a pass key. He called the police.'

'That dreadful place. I simply can't understand why Richard wanted us to stay there despite what he said.'

'What did he say?'

'Oh, I don't remember exactly, something about it seemed to... the hotel seemed to... it seemed to invite him.' She started to cry.

Giuseppe watched as the tears ran down her cheeks. Should he call a nurse? He looked around. There wasn't a nurse in sight. But he needn't have worried. When he looked back she had stopped crying and wiped away the tears with the back of her hand.

'Are you all right now?'

She nodded.

'I can come back later but maybe it would be best to get it over with now, don't you think?'

She nodded again

'Yes. Well then, there is really only one most important question I have to ask you and that is, was anybody else in the room with you?'

She opened her eyes wide to stare at him in some amazement. Her nose was running. That too was wiped with the back of her hand. He saw a box of tissues on the bedside cabinet and passed them to her. 'Why on earth should there have been someone else in the room?'

'The Hotel Phoebe does not boast the best reputation in the

world. It can at times be full of, how do you say it?' He couldn't think of how to say it so finished off with, 'some very bad peoples, yes?'

'There was no one in the room. There was just Richard and me.'

'You are quite sure.'

'Of course I'm sure! Damnit! The door was locked and...'

'Locked doors in 'otels mean nothing. They do not stop...'

'How many more times do I have to tell you? There was no one in the room but Richard and myself!'

'Please. Do not excite yourself, I'm sorry, but what I am suggesting is maybe someone crept into the room for the purpose of theft; Richard waked up and they struggled and the man fled away leaving Richard on the floor. Is that not possible?'

For a long moment she stared at him, her expression grim, then she lay back and turned away. The interview was over.

'Yes,' Giuseppe said, 'you are quite right. If that had been what happened Richard would have had bruises, maybe been cuts. Thank you for answering me and so sorry to be intrusive when you are in so sad a state. Good morning.'

Giuseppe got up, replaced the chair in its original position and left the room. There would be no need to slice Richard open from sternum to pubes. He could be sent home unmarked.

\*\*\*\*

Bunny sat in her office trying to concentrate on the work she had to get through but it was an uphill battle. Her mind was full of Enrico Agostino and all that he had said, wondering if she had heard aright or was all that praise merely to soften her up for another surprise?

There was a knock on the door and Vincenzo appeared.

'May I come in?'

'Of course.'

'Is the high and mighty one still around?'

'I've no idea. He asked permission to look around the museum, as though he needed permission, and I said of course and if there was anything he needed to let me know. In fact I offered to accompany him but he said he would rather be on his own, take his own time as it were, linger here, move fast there, depending upon interest. Okay, I said, as long as he paid his four euro but I don't think he has much of a sense of humour, in fact I can't help wondering just what goes on in that brilliant mind of his. Anyway, what are you doing here?'

'Lunch break. Thought I would have it in your cafeteria and my curiosity got the better of me. I came to find out what's going on.'

'Going on? Nothing's going on. What do you think should be going on?'

'Yes there is. What brought high and mighty around? And there's a policeman downstairs, snooping, and Francesco informs me the police were here before. Has Francesco by the way ever told you of his claim to fame?'

'No. What is his claim to fame?'

'That his father cleaned the lavatory for Mussolini and brushed the great man down when he'd had his piss? He doesn't mention whether he got a tip or not.'

'Is that a fact?'

'Probably not, but he likes to tell it and who am I to disabuse him? Well, if nothing interesting's going on, I'll go have my lunch. Or should I wait and find out what the policeman wants?'

'Go have your lunch. If what he wants proves to be interesting I'll let you know.'

'Hope he's not here to arrest you. I don't have the money to bail you out.'

Vincenzo opened the office door to leave and found Giuseppe standing there. He stood back to allow the policeman to enter. Bunny got up from behind her desk and Vincenzo, pulling a wry face and with a big shrug left, closing the door behind him. Giuseppe advanced into the room.

'Good day, Professa Coniglio. I am Inspector Giuseppe Borelli. I hope I am not disturbing you.'

'The presence of a policeman always disturbs me,' Bunny said with a smile. 'Please, take a seat, Inspector.' She indicated the chair in front of her desk.

'Thank you.'

'And tell me what all this is about.'

'To be quite frank with you, Professa, I don't really know what it is all about. I am thrashing about in a sea of uncertainty, totally bewildered.'

'I don't understand.' Bunny bit her lip trying not to laugh at the poesy. She liked this young man. More than that, she was intrigued by him. He did not strike her as to what she always thought policemen were like or, in her imagination, should be.

'Do you believe in witchcraft?' He had blurted it out before he could stop himself.

For a while there was silence as they sat looking at each other and although neither of them realised it at the time, the magic had started.

# CHAPTER 7

Sergeant Ducati had plenty of time while in hospital to think about his sudden heart attack and what had happened. Did he really see that child or was it a figment of his imagination? He never thought of himself as being the over-imaginative kind, in fact as a Taurian he was pretty much down to earth when all was said and done, not the kind to indulge in day dreams even as a kid... and yet... and yet. In his mind's eye he could still see the boy as clearly as if he were still standing in front of him. Was it merely the atmosphere in the museum that caused it? Was it a reflection from the glass of one of the enlarged photographs? One that moved? Stretched out its arms? Hardly. It was all very odd. In some strange way he almost wished he could see the child again just to make sure he really existed or wasn't simply a figment. How would he know though, if the child did reappear, that he was not a figment of his imagination? Perhaps if he could get closer to him, talk to him, maybe even touch him. No, he didn't think that was a good idea, not a good idea at all. His heart attack had certainly been no figment of the imagination. He would not like to suffer that pain again. What happened after he passed out? Did the museum curator see the child? What about his career now? Would he be considered unfit to continue in the force or would he be given the all clear? If he was not given the all clear what would he do? Police work was all he knew. That was something to really worry about; but he shouldn't worry. Worry could bring on another attack, couldn't it?

He was so lost in his thoughts he hadn't even noticed his wife had come in and was standing beside him. He looked up and, if he was smiling before, his smile was now a grin from ear to ear as he took her hand and she bent down to be kissed. He couldn't help but feel he had had a lucky escape. Now everything would turn all right; he was sure of it.

****

Bunny finally broke the silence. 'Well, Inspector… Borelli did you say?'

'Yes, Giuseppe Borelli.' He wanted her to know his first name. He hoped she would remember it.

'What is it I can do for you? I must presume it is something to do with the museum, or have I been guilty of something? Broken a few EU edicts perhaps?'

'I hope not, Signora.'

'Signorina.'

'Excuse me, Signorina.' She's not married. But surely she must have a boy friend? Maybe she's engaged. He hadn't noticed if she was wearing a ring. A woman as beautiful as this must have many admirers.

'I'm waiting, Inspector.' She was smiling.

'What?'

'How you think I can help you. What it is you want to know.'

'Oh, I'm sorry. I was, you know, gathering my thoughts.'

'You mean you hadn't gathered them before you came in? Or did they disperse when faced with this stern looking lady sitting across from you?'

Giuseppe wasn't too sure how he should react to this so decided for a moment, until he really had gathered his scattered thoughts, it was best to give no answer.

'Well, maybe if you just tell me what you are investigating,' she continued. 'That would be a good starting point, yes?'

'I am trying to tie up a few loose ends regarding the Englishman who died of a heart attack.'

Bunny frowned. 'Englishman? What Englishman? You mean the young man who was in here with his wife?'

'Yes.'

There was a moment's silence while Bunny took this in. 'A heart attack? He's dead?'

Giuseppe nodded.

'How dreadful! And the wife, is she…'

'She's in the hospital. I'm afraid she lost the baby.'

After a couple of false starts Bunny finally found her voice though it was still no more than a whisper.

'But that is terrible', she said again, 'truly dreadful.' She picked up her pencil to toy with it, looking down at her desk before looking up again. 'But, Inspector, if it was a heart attack what is there to clear up?'

'I have this feeling… something very strange…'

'A feeling? Why?'

'There have been three deaths and one near death, my sergeant who is even now in the hospital, also having suffered a heart attack. But you know all about that. You were with him at the time I believe.'

'Yes.'

'Can you tell me exactly what happened?'

'Not really. I mean there's not much to tell. I walked into the room and saw him suddenly collapse.'

'That was fortuitous. Why, if I may ask, were you going into that particular room?'

'I had some new photographs I wanted to place.'

'And, as you entered, you immediately saw him collapse?'

'Yes. Fortunately I do know about resuscitation so I could tend to him while we waited for the ambulance to arrive. And that was it.'

'The kiss of life?'

'Yes. And a good pummelling. I hope he is not too bruised.' She smiled. 'You will have to apologise for me if he is. I take it he is recovering?'

'I am pleased to say yes, thank you.' He was thinking he wouldn't half mind a bit of pummelling himself. 'There was no one else in the room when you found him?'

'No. What was he doing in the museum? Was it part of your investigation?'

'Do you not think that these deaths in such quick succession might indicate something strange is going on?'

'No. Why should it? Death comes to all of us, Inspector, one way or another. Who else, apart from the Englishman, has died and were they all heart attacks?'

'Oh, I made a mistake when I said three deaths, there have actually been four. Two of them were in an automobile accident.'

'And that doesn't surprise me, knowing how some of those boy racers drive. How did it happen?'

'The evidence points to an uncontrollable skid on a wet road with the car turning over on its bonnet a number of times and it wasn't a boy racer. Do you know a woman named Madam Rosetta?'

Bunny froze.

'No!' It came out too fast, too pat, too loud and Giuseppe knew it was a lie. However he didn't want to say something like "are you sure?" which would indicate he was aware she was lying. What was more important is why should she lie? But before he could think of a way to continue she interrupted his thoughts.

'Why would you want to know that? That I might possibly know this... this... What did you say her name was?'

'She called herself Madam Rosetta and maintained she was a clairvoyant. Did she foresee her own death do you think?'

Bunny was now very unsure of herself. Had he swallowed her lie or had he not?

'You said there were two of them. Who was the other?'

'Her daughter evidently. A young girl. Must have been very pretty before her face was crushed.' He was turning the screw. 'Oh, excuse me, and I am still mistaken. There were five deaths if you include the baby.'

Bunny nodded and turned to look out of the window for a moment before turning back. It would seem she had recovered from her initial shock at being asked about Madam Rosetta. 'It's always tragic', she said, 'when someone so young dies I mean. I'm not thinking of the baby, I mean the daughter.' She sighed. 'I'm sorry, Inspector, I don't seem to be able to help you. Was there anything else?'

'Yes. Do you believe in ghosts?'

Bunny tucked in her chin, opened her eyes very wide and laughed.

Giuseppe, impassive, sat regarding her.

'What a bizarre question, Inspector? Do I believe in ghosts? The answer to that is a big fat no. No I do not believe in ghosts.' She was pushing it too hard. 'Do *you* believe in ghosts? It really seems a very strange question for a down to earth policeman to ask.'

'A policeman I may be, Professa, but down to earth? Definitely not. You could even say I am a romantic at heart.' He was looking straight at her, smiling, and Bunny got the message. How could she miss it? She didn't want to say anything more in case she stammered. This was a totally unexpected turn of events.

'This ghost... that neither of us believes in...' His smile broadened in an attempt to put her off her guard. 'This ghost that I am led to believe at least two people have seen, possibly four if it appeared to the two women. Firstly Antonio...'

'Antonio?'

'The first policeman. Antonio Modafferi.'

'Oh, yes.'

And then Luka, Sergeant Ducati who, if I may say so is a completely down to earth policeman and who, despite the fact that he appears to be constantly smiling at some little secret of his own, really has very little imagination. So I would like to know why, before he collapsed, he saw this ghost.'

'He told you that?'

Giuseppe nodded and waited for her response. Eventually it came.

'This ghost... that neither of us believes in but which at least two people have seen... How did they describe it?'

'The interesting thing is that, though the incidents were quite far apart, the descriptions tally and, what amazes me, is that Ducati never knew of the first appearance so how did he come to describe the boy exactly as Antonio did?'

'Boy?'

'Yes, boy. Young boy. Not an Italian boy they both say, oh, in Antonio's case, said, not by the way he was dressed, but a Greek boy. Isn't that strange? Well,' Giuseppe said, getting to his feet, 'I think I've taken up enough of your time. You must have a lot to do.'

Bunny too got up and came out from behind her desk. He could see she was badly shaken which was exactly what he had meant to do and he knew somewhere in this building was the answer he was looking for.

'If you don't mind I would like to take a look around. In

particular I would like to see the room in which Luka, that is Sergeant Ducati, had his heart attack.'

'Of course. Let me take you there.'

'Please, don't inconvenience yourself. Just tell me where it is.'

'It's no trouble. No trouble at all.' Her mind was racing. There were two objects and photographs in that room she didn't want him to see, not just yet, but how to stop him?

It was Dalila who stopped him. Like a gentleman, Giuseppe had no sooner opened the office door to usher Bunny out when the girl was discovered standing there, obviously in a terrible state.

'Dalila? What's the matter? What's happened?'

'It's Francesco. I think he's dead.'

\*\*\*\*

Doctor Angelo Pettinati was a big man in every sense of the word. Hail fellow and well met; if anyone could be described as down to earth it was he. Against all medical advice he liked his food to which his bulk testified. Against all medical advice he had never done a day's exercise in his life. Against all medical advice he was not averse to a drop of alcohol. Against all medical advice he enjoyed his tobacco and now, having left his assistant to stitch up and having discarded his protective gear, he lit a welcome cigarette and inhaled deeply while he ruminated over what he had just seen. What he had just seen was now in a jar waiting to be examined further down the line but in all his long experience Angelo Pettinati had never experienced anything like it. His meditation was interrupted by the arrival of Giuseppe who wasted no time with preliminaries.

'Well?'

'Well.'

'What's the verdict?'

'Heart attack of course.' He put out his cigarette and turned to the wash basin, turned on the tap and pumped the liquid soap to wash his hands. Then he turned back and, as he dried them, continued with, 'But tell me this, Giuseppe, what kind of heart attack leaves that organ looking as though it's been through a mangle? Any ideas?' He discarded the towel and searched for another cigarette only to find the packet empty.

'You're the medical man, Angelo, what do you make of it?'

'To be absolutely frank, right this minute I don't make anything of it. I tell you, this is something I have never come across before and I somehow doubt anyone else has either. Do you want to see it?'

'I think not. I take your word for it. But what about the death certificate?'

'No problem. Like I said, definitely a heart attack.'

'At least this one was of an age when a heart attack might have been in order but there seems to have been a sudden rash of coronary failures recently and, if you keep on smoking the way you do, there will shortly be another one.'

Angelo gave his chest a hearty thump which brought on a fit of coughing. 'Sound as a bell,' he said when he had regained his breath. 'I could do with a drink and I'm all out of cigarettes. Care to join me?' He was putting on his jacket as he spoke.

Giuseppe looked at his watch. 'Why not?' He said.

****

Bunny stood facing the case that held the two heads. She still thought of them as her boys. They gazed back at her with such clear eyes and an expression of such innocence she still did not want to believe what seemed only too obvious but she was torn between her desire to ignore the evidence, circumstantial though it maybe, or to call Giuseppe and lay it all out before him. She was haunted by Madam Rosetta and the terrifying dream she had after the woman's visit. She was haunted by the deaths, Francesco being the latest and that in the museum itself, but surely this conjecture was getting her nowhere. Surely this was nothing but superstition. Could it be that two inanimate objects dug up after being buried for thousands of years could unleash an unknown and so dangerous an evil?

'Buon giorno.'

She was so engrossed she hadn't heard his approach and almost screamed out in fright at the sound of his voice. Shaking quite violently she found herself clutching at the glass cabinet for support'

'I'm sorry. I didn't mean to have startled you. Are you all right?'

Unable momentarily to find her voice she merely nodded, and then, 'I didn't hear you come in.'

He smiled. 'I guess that's pretty obvious and again I apologise.'

'What can I do for you this time?'

'Well, if you remember, last time we were interrupted by an untimely death. That was a strange thing to say. Aren't all deaths untimely? Maybe not.'

'You're wandering, Inspector.'

'Yes. I would like you to show me around, take me through the exhibits from the dig. I've had a look at that and exchanged pleasantries with your famous archaeologist friend.'

'No friend of mine I assure you.'

'He seems pleasant enough. But he didn't impart much information. He informed me a lot of the stuff has been shipped back to Rome.'

'Yes.'

'I take it you're not too pleased about that.'

'Maybe not. But there's nothing I can do about it.'

'Why were you made curator of this museum do you suppose?'

'Your guess, my dear Inspector, is as good as mine.'

'I like that.'

'You like what?'

'The dear Inspector bit.'

For the first time Bunny smiled and he followed suit.

She hurried on before he could say anything else. 'How is your sergeant, what was his name?'

'Ducati. Luka Ducati. He's up and about I'm glad to say and will be returning to duty fairly soon. But back to business, as the old saying goes. Please, take me on a guided tour around this room. For example, what is this photograph here?'

'Oh, that is the oldest object found. Look, here is the real thing.' She showed it to him in its glass case. She was aware that he was standing very close but all his attention seemed to be on the object in question.

'What exactly is it?'

'It's a curse.'

Giuseppe suddenly felt his legs grow weak. His voice was hardly above a whisper when he asked, 'Egyptian?'

'Why, yes, how did you know?'

'Madam Rosetta told me.' He was hearing those words as she had told them to him and he couldn't help but whisper them out loud, 'May you and all your children suffer. May your hearts be broken as you have broken mine.'

'Now, Inspector, surely you don't believe...'

'Yes, I do believe. I don't want to but I do. This is what she told me. She saw it all in her dreams, over and over again. A child was abducted for a sacrifice presumably to the moon goddess and as he was being taken away his mother held up that... that thing, and cursed those responsible and I believe that in digging it up somehow the curse has been reactivated, sort of like the curse of Tutankhamun maybe. What is more...' He took her by the arm and moved over to the case that held the boys' heads. '...I believe those two boys were sacrificial victims. Am I right? God only knows I don't want to be right, it is too macabre for words but it is what I am led to believe and I think now that you must believe it too.'

Bunny nodded, shook her head, nodded again.

'She wanted, no she begged me to destroy them. But I couldn't do that. How could I do that? They are beautiful, unique, priceless.'

'I understand that but the question remains, what are we going to do?'

'Inspector Borelli, what can we do? You know as well as I that if we propagated this myth in any way we would be laughed to scorn as being superstitious idiots. No, I am afraid there is nothing we can do but hope there will be no more incidents.'

'Incidents?'

'Deaths then, deaths!' She almost yelled it.

'You're willing to take that chance?'

'I have to. Now, if you'll excuse me...'

She hurried from the room. Giuseppe wondered for a moment if, in her obviously distressed state, he should follow her but decided against it. Instead he remained staring at the heads until he was suddenly aware that he was not alone. He turned around. The boy was standing no more than a few feet from him and he was smiling. It was such a seraphic smile and Giuseppe couldn't take his eyes off the small figure as it stretched out its arms towards him. And then the strangest thing happened. A man hurried into the room and threw himself virtually at the apparition's feet. It was Enrico Agostino.

'No!' He cried.

The boy turned away from Giuseppe and focused on Agostino.

'I am the one you are looking for. I am the one who took you from your mother, who led you to be sacrificed. Forgive me! It's me you want.'

The boy stretched out an arm and made a thrusting gesture with an open hand that sent Agostino flying backwards across the room to hit the wall and fall in a crumpled heap. Giuseppe ran over to him only to discover the man was dead and, as he turned him over, he saw the blood already soaking his shirt.

He turned back to face the boy who pulled aside his tunic to reveal the hole and the caked black blood on his young chest. And then, even as Giuseppe watched, seemingly mesmerised, the wound seemed to close up and disappear and the boy, whole again, started to turn into the man he would have been. And as he grew, so did the intense feeling of evil emanating from the figure, have Giuseppe literally trembling with a fear he had never before experienced. The face before him changed from the fresh pale beauty of childhood into one of such dark malevolence it was difficult for Giuseppe to believe this was actually happening, not some hideous nightmare and, as the figure with its strange blue eyes stared unblinkingly at him, he felt the sudden tightness in his chest that had him sink to his knees and he knew this was his end.

It was at that moment the earthquake struck. The floor beneath him trembled violently and, as though it were an ultimate horror, the man's head seemed to split in two, as though a cleaver had sliced it clear down the middle; and Giuseppe fainted.

****

Bunny was discovering the damage the earthquake had caused. It wasn't as bad as she had feared but the case in which the two cups, the boys' heads, were displayed had been shattered and, what was worse; the larger of the two was split straight down the middle and lay in the case in two pieces. Strange to say though, when she held the two pieces together, there seemed to be an expression of peace on the face, or did she just imagine it?

The smaller one was still intact.

www.ingramcontent.com/pod-product-compliance
Lightning Source LLC
Chambersburg PA
CBHW031336170626
46807CB00002B/723